God loves you!

Anne Greene

TIPSY IN LOVE
BY
ANNE GREENE

ISBN: 9798861197250

DEDICATION

This book is dedicated to all my readers who believe in falling in love and living happily ever after. Some people believe in love at first sight and others don't. Guess which way I believe.

As always, my book is dedicated to my own Hero husband, Colonel Larry A. Greene.

A special dedication to the Man who gave me life eternal, the Lord Jesus Christ.

SCRIPTURE

God showed us how much he loved us by sending his one and only Son into the world so that we might have eternal life through him. This is real love—not that we loved God, but that he loved us and sent his Son as a sacrifice to take away our sins.

CHAPTER 1

Charm Clearbell whacked her iced tea glass on the wooden tabletop. "I'm telling you, Flurry, I was all set for the Big Surprise! Harry and I were right here at *Our Place By The Sea*. Charm waved her hand. "Not out here on the terrace where we hear the ocean splashing against the pier, but inside in *The Crystal Room* at a secluded table by the window." She spread her hands in a flowing gesture. "The one that looks out over the largest part of the harbor where the money yachts anchor." She smiled. "Candles glowed, and Harry had ordered gorgeous red roses for our table. The place could not have been more lovely if the restaurant had been a scene in a romantic movie."

Flurry flipped slender fingers through her short-cropped dark hair. "And Harry had that tiny box I saw him leave Tiffany's with?"

"Why else does a guy shop at such an expensive jewelry store? Yes, he had the box in his hand and his hand on the table. He placed his other palm over mine and gazed into my eyes."

1

"Oooh." Flurry held her fingers in a position of prayer below her cute little chin. "Just the right setting for your new life to begin." She crinkled her nose and pointed. "But your ring finger is still bare. Did you reject Harry? Why? He's so perfect. Tall, blond, and buff. And that job of his. Plastic Surgeon. The money rolls in. Think how he can keep you looking younger each year you age!" Flurry was all but jumping up and down in her chair. "Of course, you said yes."

Charm heaved a sigh. "Since I knew he'd purchased my engagement ring, I was contemplating which surprised and radiant face to put on as you suggested." She shoved her fist against her closed lips.

"You expected a bigger diamond?"

Charm shook her head so slightly the mass of sun-kissed waves flowing below her shoulders didn't stir. "I thought Harry would go down on one knee here in the restaurant. Figured making a public show of our engagement would be just like him. I glanced around to find the photographers he'd brought to record this momentous event, but they remained well hidden."

"If you don't tell me where the ring is, I'll scream louder than these seagulls dive-bombing our table."

Charm nodded. "Harry pushed the tiny box, all wrapped in gorgeous white paper and tied with a pink bow, across the tablecloth. 'For the most beautiful woman I've ever known.'" His brown eyes danced and the skin around them wrinkled. 'And I've been acquainted with more than my share.'"

Flurry furrowed her brow. "That's a twisted compliment."

Charm bit her lip until the tender flesh hurt. "But of course, he has. He's transformed a slew of women from attractive to spectacular." She formed her lips into a tiny smile. "But Harry chose me." She pulled in a deep breath. "Well, I tell you, when I saw that beautiful ring box, my whole body tingled. Finally, after almost a full year of dating, Harry realized he couldn't go on living without me. I felt happy. Content. Mission accomplished. And none too soon. The old clock is ticking. In a few months I'll celebrate twenty-seven years on Planet Earth. I don't want to be like so many women today and add to our country's depopulation crisis. Nor do I want to freeze my eggs while I further my career."

"Yes, you want to utilize your eggs while they're still fresh." Flurry shook her head, her hazel eyes going dreamy. "My engagement ring might be small, but I'm so in love with my Freddie."

Charm clutched her throat. "Mmm."

"So, your whopper is in the jewelry shop to resize?"

"Not exactly."

"I'm all giddy with goosebumps. Where is that diamond?"

Charm cleared her throat. "I settled on my I'm-so-in-love-with-you-and-this-gift-is-such-a-surprise-face. I reverently took the tiny box and almost hated to untie the delightful pink ribbon and bow. My hand actually trembled when I removed the lid." Charm's throat closed. She sipped her glass of mango iced tea.

Flurry slipped from the high wooden chair, planted her feet in front of Charm, and pounded the tall table with both fists. "Girl, you tell me where the engagement ring is!"

People sitting at other tables glanced at them.

Charm dropped her head. "I opened the box and screamed. I tried to convert the scream into a yelp of delight, but it was too late."

"Harry grabbed the edges of the table. 'Don't you like the diamond earrings?'"

"I could barely hear Harry's voice over the ringing in my burning ears." When my wits returned, I bleated, "Yes. Yes, they are lovely."

"'Well, put them on.'" Harry had that rather aggravated expression he wears when he's in charge, but his PAs aren't kowtowing."

"My fingers were clumsy when I took off my excellent cubic zirconias and inserted the genuine diamonds. The gems from Harry *were* larger."

Flurry's sympathetic, wide-eyed stare boosted Charm to continue. "The biggest diamond earrings I'd ever seen. Harry spent a ton of money on them. So surely, he loves me."

"*Adores* you more like. Who wouldn't? You've got that mischievous sparkle to you that no man can resist. And you're every man's dream with those enormous blue eyes and incredible shining hair. I can't even grow my thatch that long. And everyone knows abundant hair is a sign of ripe fertility." A tiny frown flitted across Flurry's Cafe Latte-colored face, then her normal, sunny expression returned. "And that smile of yours. How many other ladies pose for their dentist's publicity photo?"

"But Harry sees beautiful women every day."

"Yeah. Gals who look far better when he's done with them." Flurry shook her finger. "Nope, he's found a natural beauty. And he's not about to let you go. Why, those earrings yell, you belong to me."

Charm tilted her head. "Do you really think so? I thought an *engagement ring* said *I want you to be mine forever*."

Flurry rounded back to her seat and climbed up. "Don't worry, Dr. Face-changer will get around to the right diamond."

Charm took a long swig of iced tea. She stirred the straw in the ice, making the small clear cubes tinkle. "But there's more."

"No."

"Harry admitted the earrings are a token for me because he has to leave Tampa for an extended stay in Scotland. Evidently, he has family there, and they've arranged for him to visit. And he's to teach a medical course near Inverness."

"Well, the earrings are a nice gift."

"He'll be out of the country three months."

"Ooh kaaay."

"You realize in three months I'll be twenty-seven. My mother birthed me when she was twenty-one. Grandma had Mom when she was nineteen." Charm shrugged. "And look at you, barely twenty-three, and my last unmarried friend. And you have your sweet Freddie." Charm struggled to hold back her ugly, crying face and finally won. She sniffed.

"So, what are you going to do?"

"What can I do? Lose myself in my job and pray Harry won't meet a darling Scottish lassie."

Flurry shook her head, her hazel eyes serious. "Fear doesn't sound like you, Charm. You're the go-for-the-goal gal. In a very competitive field, you're a successful corporate travel agent. You're proactive. You're a modern woman." She dragged her over-large hobo purse from the back of her chair, delved inside for her compact, applied shine, and thumped the purple bag on the table. "The way I see the situation, you've got two options."

A warm flush splashed Charm from face to neck. She straightened and thrust out her chest. "Right. I must act. Do something." She gazed out to where waves paddled against the anchored yachts and gave a small groan. "What choices?"

Flurry chopped her hand in the air. "One, cut your losses and break up with Harry."

"But I think I'm in love with him."

"Right. That brings us to the second choice. Love makes the guy worth fighting for." Flurry shook her finger in Charm's direction. "Number two, go after Harry."

"What?" The heat deepened and spread down to her chest. Chase a man? Never. With all the men she'd dated, she'd never had to pursue one. Not a single one. Only losers took such drastic measures. Women with no hope.

"You said you love him. And he isn't just any man. He's Harry Bear, the eminent Plastic Surgeon."

"That's true." The flush dripped further down her body and leaked out through her sparkling silver toenails. Charm thrust both elbows on the table and tucked her chin into her hand.

"Don't you have a B & B or a lodge or a hotel in Scotland you need to check out in-person-on-site?"

"I've never travelled to Scotland." Charm shifted in her chair and rubbed her empty ring finger. "But quite a few clients have expressed an interest in visiting there. I never pursued that venue."

"Where is Harry teaching?"

"The Academy of Plastic Surgeons at Inverness."

"Where is Inverness?"

"I'm not sure. I checked on the internet and discovered the town is in the Highlands."

"Easy. Find a B & B there and bump into him."

"Harry wouldn't be fooled. He'd immediately know meeting him wasn't accidental."

Flurry's eyes lit with a devious glow. "Tell him this is Leap Year. And you're asking him to marry you."

"That's as subtle as a ton of muddy bricks. There has to be a better way. And yet, Harry has already spoken of several Scottish maidens as being absolute natural beauties. Why do women like that need a plastic surgeon anyway?"

Flurry leaned across the small table. "A Scottish brogue on melodious lips is dreadfully alluring. And three months' absence can make a man forget. Not that Harry's wishy-washy, but one-fourth of a year is a long time. Anything can happen."

Finding she couldn't speak, Charm nodded.

"Didn't the leap year tradition start in Scotland?" Flurry's hazel eyes widened. "I'm certain the tradition started in Scotland. In 1828 Queen Margaret of Scotland introduced a law allowing women to propose during leap year. She also penalized men who refused a leap year proposal." Flurry's mouth twisted into a wry smile. "Or was it in Scotland that men kidnapped women to be their brides? Oh well, everyone knows leap year is when every woman proposes to the man she loves."

Charm slipped her credit card on top of the check and motioned to the handsome waiter. Larry nodded and took her credit card. "Thank you, as always, Charm." He smiled at Flurry. "And you too, Miss." He squared his muscular shoulders and moved away.

Charm tapped her fingers on the table. True enough, this was leap year. Not that she needed that excuse. When she made up her mind, she didn't need a silly tradition to pursue Harry. *If* she decided to go after him.

And yet, with Harry's big personality, he might like being pursued.

Or he might not.

Weren't all men egotists when faced with wanting the attention of women?

Flurry was right. Once she made her decision, she was a Pit Bull. Not a woman to be trifled with.

Or so she told herself.

So, which option was she crazy enough to take?

TIPSY IN LOVE

CHAPTER 2

Charm pushed her way through the crowd at the Aberdeen airport. Now that she had made up her mind, a summer burst of awful storms would not keep her from her goal. Surely there were other modes of transportation to Inverness. This late in August, she had only a few months before leap year ended and her proposal window closed.

She had to reach Inverness before she lost her nerve.

Being grounded in Aberdeen would not alter her plans. No, she couldn't wait until the end of the week for this storm to pass. During his last phone call, Harry had mentioned giving private tutoring lessons to a lass named Colleen. What could be more attractive than a husband- and-wife-run surgery unit? Harry was not a person to overlook a winning opportunity.

Back home she knew of no women who were plastic surgeons. Was Scotland so far ahead?

She bounced from one foot and then the other, until, at last, no one stood between her and the lady tending the airport counter.

The woman, wearing the uniform with the blue and white national colors of Scotland, brushed her light brown hair back from her tired-looking face. "How may I help you, Miss?"

Charm tried not to let panic seep into her voice. "I need a ticket to Inverness, please. Any seat. I must leave today."

"I'm sorry, but there are no flights in or out of this airport for at least three more days. The last plane that landed came from overseas and, with the wind and rain so bad, barely stayed on the runway."

"Frightening landing. Yes, I know. I was on that plane. The destination was Inverness, but we were diverted here. But since we landed safely, I'm certain there must be a flight out of here directly to Inverness. I need a seat on that flight."

The lady in line behind Charm nudged her shoulder. "Hurry up, please. We've been waiting almost all night to book a flight out."

Charm turned her back on the agitated lady. "There must be a flight to somewhere. A flight that heads west in the same direction as Inverness?"

The airline agent's brow puckered. "I'm sorry, Miss. As I said. there are no flights out. Now please step aside."

Charm glanced back over her shoulder, then gazed around the crowded room. People and baggage clumped everywhere. Some folks, draped over the hard bench seats, slept with heads and bodies slumped over what had to be another member of their party. Other people sprawled on spread-out coats on the floor next to piled luggage. Eyes wide, a few dogs lay panting next to their masters. A piteous meow emitted from a small cage tucked between two trunks. There was scarcely room to take two steps between massed people.

"How long has this storm been raging?"

"Look Miss, I've been behind this counter for two days. There's nothing I can do. This is what some weatherman calls *A Perfect Storm*. We've seen nothing like this in my lifetime. We don't even know how much longer the deluge will last." The woman waved a hand. "Next!"

Charm stepped out of line. This weather wouldn't stop her. Perfect Storm indeed. She'd seen worse in … well not in Tampa. Hurricanes, yes. But in the U.S. a downpour like this wouldn't have halted transportation. There must be some way to circle around the cloudburst. She eyed the room, small for an airport, but she'd been in smaller … like the airport in Totola, B.V.I. A storm wouldn't have stopped the English from functioning. Nor the Germans. Were the Scots less hardy?

She had to find other transportation.

At the far end of the room near the exit a line of men held various signs at chest level. Oh, yes, escorts meeting people disembarking. Perhaps one of them was going her way.

She headed in that direction, silently reading their signs as she pushed her way through the crowd. *Nairn, Badenoch, Strathspey. Institute for Gaelic Language Studies.*

Where were those places? Not a single sign read *Inverness.* Why hadn't she researched the country before she made her last-second trip to Scotland? Ha, who would have expected a storm to reroute her plane?

She stepped around a man, woman, and little

girl lying on a blanket together, blissfully asleep in this chaos. Well, she was an independent woman, and she would not spend however many nights stuck in this dismal airport. She had absolutely no vacation time left this year, so she must track down Harry before the end of August and return to Tampa ASAP. And she *would* be wearing that ring.

Charm smiled. She and Harry could have a Christmas wedding. Tampa was beautiful at Christmastime, alight with decorations, and with strings of gorgeous white lights lining all the streets, especially by the waterfront. She and Harry could marry in her church and reserve the party room at *Our Place By The Sea* for their reception. She would have red bridesmaids' gowns.

All she needed was to escape this over-crowded, noisy, damp, slightly musty smelling airport and be on her way to Harry.

She tugged her over-night bag through the mass of humanity sprawled in her way and approached the line of men gazing half-heartedly at the entrance door. Since the last of the passengers from her plane disembarked at least twenty minutes ago, no new person entered. The men were turning away and shuffling off in different directions.

"Wait!" She shivered at the shrill of her cry, like that of an eagle diving for a running rabbit. She held up the hand not clutching her rolling overnight bag.

Eyes wide, mouths open, several men gazed back. The rest continued on as if they had not heard her piercing cry. Only one fella stopped and faced her. A grizzled oldster with a snowy beard and mustache that covered half his face. A Santa look-alike, dressed from head to toe in a raincoat with the hood pushed back.

"Yes, Ma'am?" His deep voice resonated through the crowd causing two of the dispersing men to turn back.

She addressed the three of them, her voice as loud as an intercom announcement. "I would so appreciate a ride to the train station."

The two cowards spun around and fled toward the exit.

Rude.

The oldster with the silver beard frowned. "Sorry, I am, to be the bearer of ill news, young lady, but the River Don and the River Dee be flooded and those on this side canna get ta the other." He stroked his beard. Besides the train 'tisn't running, due to the flood.

"What?"

"The way ta the station is blocked. Water is waist-high and none with good sense would go that way, except by canoe." He winked a twinkling, blue eye.

"What about a bus to Inverness?"

"Bus station parks next ta the train station." He twitched his nose. "And I hear the busses stopped running just afore the storm broke."

Charm forced herself not to stamp her foot. Was God trying to tell her something? "In that case," she unhooked her purse from its spot rubbing a cleft into her shoulder, opened the bag, and drew out her wallet. "If I can't leave by train or bus, do you have a car? Can you drive me?" She joked,

"You're not an axe murderer, are you?"

The silver head nodded. "Aye. I could drive ye."

"But?"

"Me transportation may not be ta yer liking."

"I must get to Inverness. I have urgent business there."

The man looked her up and down and rubbed his chin. His stooped shoulders straightened a bit. "I could get ye to Inverness, but we'd have ta take a slight detour, ye see."

"Slight?"

"A few wee miles. I'll leave the price ta your charity as I was heading that way meself."

"But your sign says, Fraserburgh?"

"Aye. Fraserburgh. Just a few wee miles north of Inverness. Ye might say jist a hop, skip, and a duck waddle further north. Then you travel down the coast ta Inverness."

"You know the way?"

"I do. Born and grew up in this area, Lassie."

"You'll drive me in this storm?"

"Aye, Lass. In me day, I've seen far worse."

Ha, at last someone with sense. "My bag is still in luggage. Would you mind bringing it?"

The man, face grooved into a huge grin, tucked his sign into his backpack, heaved the straps over his shoulders, and like a linebacker, hurtled a path through the crowd.

Her bag sat alone on the revolving luggage carousel.

The old man slapped a hand to his forehead. "Tis a big suitcase."

Charm smiled. "Yes, I'm in Scotland on a special mission, and I need to dress to impress."

The old man shouldered a larger man standing with his back to the luggage revolver. "Mind giving me a hand?" He nodded to Charm's oversized bag.

"Sure, glad 'tis I am to help." The Samaritan hefted the bag off the stilled carousel, and her new luggage thumped to the concrete floor. "Had to pay extra for this one, did ya? Is it full of rocks? We have rocks in Scotland."

Heat flared in Charm's cheeks, but she spun away from the young man and spoke to the old man. "Can you handle my luggage?"

He caressed his moustache. "How about ye tote the big one, and I take care of this one?" He nodded to her overnight suitcase. Without waiting for an answer, he surged forward through the crowded room, tugging her overnight case after him.

She had no choice. She shoved her over-sized luggage ahead of her as a buffer and managed to keep him in sight. He walked fast for an old fella.

Once outside, rain slapped her. She pulled her hood over her head. Why hadn't she bought a heavier raincoat? August was supposed to be warm and dry in Scotland. This was neither. But she was on her way. Soon she'd be with Harry, and this nightmare travel would be over.

She could barely see the man ahead, sloshing through ankle-deep water, her overnight bag plowing through pools like a swimmer desperate to nab a gold medal. How far was his car?

She rounded a deep-looking eddy, and her high heels sank into mud. Muck! And these were her second-best heels. The mud sucked at her shoes, but the slender straps held, and she walked like a drunken stork, wielding her heavy suitcase.

Up ahead the man had stopped. "Here we are."

"Where?" Surely not that open-air tourist bus? The ratty top didn't provide the leather seats much shelter from the rain. "You don't expect us to make the trip in that?"

"Aye, Lass. Molly Me Girl here knows the roads. She's sturdy and gets me and me passengers wherever we want ta go. Hop in."

Her mouth dropped as she watched him heave her over-night case inside on the floor behind the driver's seat. Then he reached for her big bag, and as if the oversized luggage were as light as a feather, tossed her bag aboard. He held out his dripping hand. "In you go."

Was sitting, barely sheltered from the pelting rain, in the rickety bus better than dying from pent-up frustration inside the overcrowded airport? Maybe not. But at least she would be getting to her destination. Her high heel slipped on the step, and Santa head-butted her rear to boost her up into the bus.

Whoops that wasn't pretty. Glad no one saw that move. Charm tucked the hood of her light raincoat back up over her dripping hair and snuggled into a seat in the middle where less rain blew in from the open sides. "How long is the ride?"

Santa, climbing inside the more protected cab, glanced back. "Jist a wee way. We'll be there before ye can count the raindrops." He leaned forward and turned the key in the ignition. The engine growled, stalled, coughed, and then burst into life. A loud backfire.

Charm started, then glanced around. Nothing to see except slashing rain, a small, dismal airport building whose bright lights now seemed far friendlier than the darkness surrounding the bus. Was accepting this ride a mistake? Should she go back inside? Too late. The bus jerked, rumbled, and bounced forward, leaving the airport behind so quickly the building seemed a dream.

Charm curled her body together, tenting her raincoat over every inch of herself except her bare toes protruding from the straps of her high heels. Dry and warm the guidebook said. She shivered. Not too cold, just chilly. And not drowning in water thanks to the tattered roof and her raincoat. And Santa promised a short ride.

~

Ow! That rut was so deep her whole body bounced on the wet seat. She held tight to the handrail that backed the cab and fronted the bus seat. Her hands ached from gripping the bar. This was ridiculous. She'd been bouncing along this road more than a half hour and as yet seen nothing. No lights. No houses. No stores. Nothing but darkness. How far was a wee way?

"Hey," she screamed. Why hadn't she asked Santa his name. "How much longer?"

He turned so far back in his seat toward her she feared he would drive off the road. The lights from the dashboard reflected his silver hair and beard. "Just a wee way."

Bam! The bus hit a deep rut, sank in axle deep, and jolted to a halt.

"Whoa, Molly! That was a big 'un." He twisted even further in his seat, craned his neck, and faced her. "Jist a jiffy, and I'll have her runnin' again. She's a reliable old gal, but she doesn't like this storm." He hopped out his door and moved to the rear of the bus.

"Oh, dear God, what now?" Charm prayed. "Please get this bus started again." Ahead she saw twinkling lights. "Are we here?" she called to Santa.

She could barely make out his form in the darkness as he unbent and shuffled over to lean inside the bus.

"If I can get Molly Me Girl out of this ditch, we'll be on our way. See those lights ahead? That's where we be going."

"Thank you, God."

Santa climbed back into the bus, shoved in the clutch, and yanked the bus into gear. The engine blasted, the tires squealed, the bus wiggled sideways, but slowly climbed out of the ditch like a fat caterpillar. "And we're off!" the cheery voice floated back.

"Hooray!" Not like her to show her feelings so easily, but nothing about this trip was like her. Where had her sense and caution fled? Probably she'd left them back in her jewelry box with those over-sized diamond earrings. She straightened her shoulders. This blip in her life she would view as an adventure. She wouldn't think of this trip as a desperate quest. Not a final, all-out attempt to marry the man she loved and to have a baby with him before her eggs crumbled into clumps of unusable cells. This was her Swan Song. Her greatest achievement. Her—

Bam! The bus lurched to a dead stand-still.

She pitched forward, knocking her chin against the back of Santa's seat. "Ow!"

Again, Santa crawled out of his cab and leaned into the bus. "Sorry, Miss. This be the end of the road. I think yer weight be too heavy for Molly Me Girl. She don't usually stop for ruts, but she's telling me 'tis time for ye ta disembark."

"You're leaving me out here in the middle of nowhere?"

"By the stars, Miss, no. This be your destination." He pointed toward the twinkling lights. "That's Fraserburgh. Ye can walk inta town from here."

"But it's raining."

"Aye, that tis."

"But my bags."

"Ah. About that, Miss. I'm afraid I have a wee bit of bad news for ye."

Charm lifted a hand to touch her throat, which somehow as Santa talked, had closed and she had a hard time swallowing. "More bad news?"

"Aye, Miss. I noted when Molly Me Girl got stuck the first time that yer wee bit of luggage had somehow managed ta escape me bus."

"What?"

"Now, now. Don't ye fret." He raised a calming hand. "Nothin' to upset yerself about. Someone'll be along come daylight, see that big bag sitting in the middle of the road, and bring it on up to Fraserburgh. We Scots do such things, ye know."

"But however will someone find me?"

"Not ta worry. 'Tis a wee town. Ye'll be found soon enough." He grabbed her overnight bag and hoisted it from behind her seat to the muddy, rain-splashed ground. "The sooner yer on yer way, the sooner ye get warm and dry." He held out his wet hand.

She stared at the hand inviting her from her relatively dry spot to venture into the raging storm. She shook her head. She could turn stubborn and stay put.

"Hot tea and a warm bath." Santa enticed.

She grasped his slippery hand, slid across the seat, and climbed down. Her spiked heels sank into deep water. Had to be at least fifty yards to the nearest lights glimmering through the pelting rain. She was already soaked. What was a wee bit more water?

CHAPTER 3

Charm landed in a puddle up to her calves. No sense trying to wheel her bag through this flood. She hefted the heavy case up in one hand, balanced her shoulder bag, and used her other hand in a vain attempt to shield her eyes from the smacking rain.

With a wave of his hand, Santa Look Alike jumped into his cab seat, cranked on the engine of his Molly Me Girl and lurched forward, the rear wheels sending a tsunami of water over her. Soon the taillights disappeared in the monsoon.

She sighed as the rear lights of the tattered bus vanished into lonely darkness, then stepped forward sloshing through water. And hit a rock. And turned her ankle. Darn, that hurt. Would her favorite high heels survive until she reached the clustered houses up ahead sending out ever-so-welcome beams of light? She reached down and slipped off one shoe, caught her balance, and removed the other. She pushed the shoes into her coat pockets. Yuck. Her bare feet had better traction in the mud below the water, but now the water rose thigh-high. The hem of her summer dress clung to her legs.

She floundered toward the light. The longer she trudged, the farther away the glow seemed. If she shouted would someone inside the building run out to help her? She shook her head. Probably no one would hear her in this gully-washer. Her water-logged hood slipped down to settle an extra ton of wetness on her neck.

She reached what, in the darkness, looked like a low stone fence enclosing a yard. She turned in the open gate. A few dozen more steps, and she knocked on the sturdy wooden door.

No answer.

Music and the sound of voices wafted through the door.

She pounded louder.

Still no answer.

She pushed against the old-fashioned door latch. The door swung open so easily she fell through onto a wooden floor. Ouch. She shook her head and water flew like a dog shaking after a bath.

A tomb-like silence replaced the music and voices.

She blinked against the bright light and struggled up from her knees. Sure enough a sign above a long wooden bar read *Fraserburgh Diner.*

She pulled in a deep breath, plunked her overnight bag onto the wooden floor, and glanced around. This was no ordinary step back in time. *Fraserburgh Diner* must have been restored to represent a tavern built for the life of a fisherman and his parents … and their parents before him. The four walls were decorated with fishing paraphernalia – baited fishing lines, items for curing, smoking, salting, and drying fish. And other implements of torture. Not exactly a place inviting to a tourist. But a steady floor beneath her feet rather than a bouncing bus felt good.

"Ho, look what the storm floated in." The resounding voice came from behind the wooden bar that took up half the small room.

"Hello." Her voice sounded as breathless as she felt. She pulled in several deep breaths.

"Sounds American."

That brogue drifted from one of the four men seated at the bar, each staring over his shoulder at her. Could they gawk anymore?

A giggle burbled up. Four stooges? One bald, one fat, one skinny, and one grinning like a Jack-O-Lantern with a missing front tooth. Friendly looking.

"Drowned rat, more like." The voice behind the bar had slightly lowered in amplification, but still several decibels above a normal-sounding male voice. "Have you lost your way ... and your shoes?"

"Neither thank you. I know precisely where I am. And my shoes are in my coat pockets." Charm softened her curt tone. "This is the *Fraserburg Diner* is it not?" Somehow her disappointment at the place, and her frustration at the day's delays had crept into her voice.

"Do all Americans stow their shoes in their coats?" Now the barkeep's tone sounded belligerent. "At your service, Miss."

Oh, the man was a piece of work. "Do all Scotsmen forget their manners?"

She shook herself, leaving a puddle under her bare feet. She unbuttoned her raincoat, swung the

24

waterlogged garment out and draped it over the nearest chair. She bent and tugged her high heels from the wilted pockets. As she slipped them on her feet a loud wolf-whistle skirled from behind the bar.

She jerked upright. So rude. "Are all Scotsman wolves at heart?"

The bald man lounging in the first seat at the bar swung around to face her, his back to the barkeep. "Now Angus Broderick McDougal, is that the way we Scots treat a lady?"

"And do you see what she's done to my clean floor?" The sarcastic voice belonged to the Scot behind the bar apparently named Angus. "And you call that a lady?"

"Sure, and Angus, the lady's dress be wet enough to show her femininity. But a gentleman wouldna make no mention of such."

Charm glanced down. Then snatched up her raincoat and wrapped the dripping thing around her body. "Mr. McDougal, you are no gentleman. In America we have a name for people like you."

"What's that?"

"Scotsmen!"

"Right you are." McDougal swung around to face away. But made no attempt to hide the grin that had spread over his face.

Charm shivered under the dripping wetness. "Could you at least direct me to a phone?"

"Phone? What phone?" Though his back remained turned, his voice sounded lazy now ... and amused. "Haven't had a land line since the storm began. But I can offer you a hot cup of coffee ... and a towel or two." He reached down behind the bar, and came up with an armful of large, taupe brown towels. He rounded the bar and strode to her. "Nor do we ever have cell service around here."

Of course they wouldn't out here in the sticks. She flipped wet hair out of her eyes. McDougal was fairly tall and medium build, dressed in nondescript pants and a worn gray sweater. Silhouetted against the light, she wouldn't recognize him if she met him on a sunny street. But his unwelcome attitude exasperated her to her last nerve, giving her voice the chill of the outside storm. "Thank you."

She snatched the wonderful, dry towels from his outstretched hands. "I'd appreciate that coffee. Now if you and the other men would be kind enough to turn your backs, I'll wrap myself in these towels." This place had all the charm of a mud dauber's nest.

"We *gentlemen* would be only too happy to gaze at something more heartening."

Ha, so her barb had hit home. Good. He may as well know she could dish out as much as she got from him. She certainly was not going to direct any of her clients to this hole-in-the-wall. This diner didn't even qualify as campy.

"Ach, speak for yerself, Angus. We haven't seen anything so nearly interesting in a good long while. Long as I can recollect," the fat man murmured.

"Aye," three other voices echoed. "Can we turn now?"

"If you must." Wrapped from neck to calf in the towels, Charm pulled an ancient chair from beneath a scarred wooden table and collapsed. Her feet hurt. She must have bruised them on the road. Every bone ached. "I've had a long, immensely irritating journey. Where is that coffee?"

"If your majesty will allow me to serve her, I will fetch her drink."

Oh, the bartender was insufferable. How did such a man run a restaurant? "Please." She laid her head on the table.

A rustle behind her and coffee, slopped over into the saucer, was placed near her hand. She didn't look up. Footsteps walked away.

She raised her head.

Because of the poor light, the barkeep was a shadow behind the bar. The four men, still inspecting her, murmured together.

Not her concern. She sipped the coffee, hot. The aromatic brew warmed her. At least the coffee was good here. The towels were warm. After the journey she'd had, sitting here, almost naked, wrapped from neck to toes in brown towels large enough to be used at a beach, seemed perfectly normal.

The four Scots at the bar kept up a continuous low babble, soothing in contrast to the muted thunder and occasional flashes outside. The barkeep, Angus, rattled dishes. No one sat at the other three tables. The room was dim as a cave. She yawned.

"Is there an inn nearby?" Her question brought immediate silence to the room as if she'd told them a bomb was about to explode. "A B & B? A cabin?"

"Humph." The four heads swiveled toward the barkeep.

He cleared his throat. Placed a glass he was drying on the wooden top of the bar.

"It's not a difficult question. I need a place to find something to eat, take a shower, and get some sleep. Surely there's such a place in Fraserburgh."

All four gaped at her, each with a different expression of surprise on his unshaven face. They looked at one another. Then, as if cued by an unseen hand, all pointed their noses at the barkeep.

He lifted a glass and wiped.

"Oh, no. Let me guess. *This* is Frasersburgh's Diner *and Inn.*" At least she wouldn't have to go out into the rain again. But what kind of room could a place like this offer?

As if they played in a comic movie the four heads pivoted to gaze at her and then at the barkeep.

McDougal slapped his dish towel on the bar, made a face as if he ate something disagreeable, swirled the dish towel on the bar top, heaved a sigh, grabbed her overnight case, then motioned for her to follow him.

Well, she'd never heard that Scots were particularly hospitable, but that man must hate women. How could such a crab run an inn? She picked up her wet dress and shoes but left her still dripping raincoat draped over two of the chairs. As she was placing each foot on a stair tread, following the bar grouch up a steep flight of steps, she overheard one of the men below.

"Nae, I didna think old Angus would let her stay."

"Nor I, after what happened to him."

Charm turned and leaned down to hear more.

Mumbling floated up.

She had to go on upstairs or rouse the barkeep's suspicions that she eavesdropped. She stepped to the landing.

The man in front of her opened a door at the top of the stairs.

She gazed around. This seemed to be the only room upstairs. Where were the others?

McDougal motioned her inside. "The sheets are clean. Changed just an hour past. There's not much space in the closet." He stalked to a chair and snatched up a jacket and a pair of boots lying nearby. "Try not to use all the hot water." He turned, stomped from the room, and slammed the door.

How odd. But this was backwoods Scotland. Life had to be different here. She peeled off the towels and hung them over the single chair. She plopped on the bed. Fairly comfortable with an inviting brown comforter over fresh scented sheets. Was everything in this inn brown? So not her favorite color. The mahogany headboard looked old-fashioned and slightly scratched. Shabby brown curtains hung at a small window. How did the untidy man run a diner? Not going to get any five stars from her.

After a hot shower, she donned the yoga clothes she always carried in her overnight suitcase and sank on the bed. Her tummy rumbled. No phone. She'd have to run downstairs and order room service. She moved to the armoire which served as a closet. Probably no slippers provided, but she'd have a look. The door creaked as she opened it. What?

The sandalwood scent of male sprang out. Mens clothes filled the small space. Men's shoes overflowed the floor space. What?

Oh no! The barkeep lived up here. This was *his* room. She twirled around to gaze at the room again. The testy, sarcastic man had a heart after all. He realized she had no other place to go and gave her his room. She blinked. This was not the bar grump she had grown to dislike. She'd have to pay him well. Yet, to be fair to her clients, still no five stars.

A knock on the thick door.

She padded barefoot and opened it.

The Jack-O-Lantern man from the bar carried a tray. Tantalizing smells wafted up. "Angus sent this." He tried to hide his gaze behind his hand, but he eyed her up and down, his smile welcoming.

She took the tray, pivoted, and laid the napkin-covered meal on the bed. "Thank him for me, please. Does he live—?"

"Angus said you used all the hot water in his hoosie."

"Hoosie?"

"Aye." The man rubbed his hands and grinned as if something tickled him. "Ye might jist be the lassie to make him stay."

"What do you mean?"

He raised and wiggled his fisted hands as if in a cheer. "Ach. Soon enough ye'll know." He laughed. Turned and took the stairs down two at a time.

Strange. Why would she want to make the eccentric man stay anywhere? Didn't he like this old tavern either? These Scots were peculiar people.

Yet she liked them.

Rain blasted against the small windowpane. She had to get to Harry.

She'd find a ride out of here tomorrow. Storm or flood. She was not made from sugar.

CHAPTER 4

Rick opened his eyes. Angus, they insisted on calling him Angus. He groaned. His back ached like a steamroller had flattened him. He pushed up from the floor. Long night. He'd not slept on the floor since he was six, and his older brothers kicked him out of bed.

He glanced around the room. His four freeloaders had each taken a table and chairs to create various beds. Snores blasted from each in a cacophony of different rackets. Sounded like a parade of oinkers rooting for grub. They'd want breakfast. And so would she.

Wheesht! She! He was not a superstitious man, but when the storm dropped her into his place last night, he'd been struck dumb. Even looking as pitiful as a drowned kitten, the woman was spectacular. Danger padding in on bare feet. A Sabrina. A storm goddess. He didn't believe in such things, but he'd never seen her equal … and he'd observed almost all of her through that short dress clinging to her skin like plastic wrap.

He shook his head. He dreamed about her last night. Not good. Really, really not good. Too much trouble in his life now for her to add to his torment.

Not with Katherine making her demands. He'd learned a lot from that Scottish lass. And none of the lessons good.

He stretched his back. Hot potatoes. That's what women were. Looked delicious and alluring on the outside, but inside, hidden under all the butter and chives … hot. Too hot to handle.

He moved into the tiny kitchen abutting the bar. Took out all the items he needed for a logger's breakfast and fired up the skillet.

Seumas stuck his bald head into the room. "How's it going back there, Angus?"

"Breakfast will be ready in about fifteen."

"Ye want I should wake the lassie?"

"Sure. The sooner she's up and eaten, the sooner she'll be on her way."

"I might be old, Angus Broderick, but in me day, I didn't let someone like that up and leave."

Rick cracked eggs into a bowl and reached for the whisk. "You would if –"

"Aye, right. I forgot about yer troubles." Seumas ran a hand over his bald head. "But this one might be different."

"She's beautiful, brash, and independent. I don't see any difference."

"Ach, give the bonnie lass a chance—"

"I've got one wildcat on my hands. I don't need another." Rick slapped strips of bacon on the ancient grill.

"Missing a good thing. How ye plan to get rid of her? Going to take the 'copter?"

Rick rolled his eyes and shrugged. "Go on. Wake her."

~

Charm smiled at the men overflowing the diner. Like a locker room filled with sweaty football players. Wonderful how morning light made a situation bearable—even humorous. She'd had a great night's sleep.

She sat down to share one of the tables with three of the men she'd seen last night. The bald man carried out plates of steaming eggs, bacon, and toast. He pulled up another chair and scrunched in to join their table. As they ate, each introduced himself and gave her a bit of his history. The fat one was Fergus, the tall, skinny one was Duncan, the bald one was Seumas, the Jack-O-Lantern one was Dougal. No sign of Angus. The four local Scots kept up a lively conversation teasing one another like long-time friends. They lived in the neighborhood, but the storm had kept them captive inside the diner. They didn't mention the man they had called Angus Broderick McDougal.

She shrugged. Not her concern. However, she liked these jovial Scots. Happily, the dour one didn't make an appearance. Yet, she couldn't help asking, "Um, Duncan, where did the man you call Angus spend the night? Are there other rooms?"

The skinny man's eyes widened. "Angus? Oh well … Sorry it 'tis, Miss Clearbell, I have me duties." He pushed back from the table and rushed for the kitchen.

Wacky. She dabbed her mouth with her napkin, rose, and strolled to the small front window. Outside the day looked dreary enough to make the small room seem cheerful. But the rain had turned into a drizzle. Surely, a little trickle wouldn't keep her from finding a ride to Inverness.

She moved back to the table. The tall, skinny man, Duncan, had returned and carried dirty dishes from the table balanced on his arm and in his hands as if he were a practiced waiter. And perhaps he was. "Um, Duncan—"

The dishes wavered. He did a balancing dance, but too late. All the dishes crashed to the wooden floor, smashed into shards, and slithered across the room.

Had her question caused him to lose control? She bent to pick up pieces, her wrinkled skirt too snug. She managed to reach one broken cup.

The other two men were at her side, one plucking her arm, the other holding out his hand. "We'll take care of this mess. Ye sit down, lassie."

Her knee-length skirt had shrunk until the dress was almost too short to wear. Almost. But it *was* too constricted for stooping. She took Dougal's hand and slipped back into her chair. The men had been chatterboxes until she'd asked about Angus. Now, they seemed struck dumb. Scots were a quirky lot.

All four men worked at cleaning the mess as if they ran a sprint to see who could finish first and scurry off to the kitchen.

She glanced around the empty room. Perhaps the land line worked today. So annoying to be so far from cell service.

Angus Broderick McDougal strode in, his boots clomping on the floor like rowdy children.

Charm sucked in a breath. A first shaft of light beamed in through the front window and spotlighted Angus, transforming his brown hair blond, his stormy eyes sunny, and his last-night's grumpy expression in a striking visage like a bold Viking or … or a medieval knight. Hmm. How had she missed recognizing that the man was fairly good-looking in a rugged way, if you liked a strong jaw on a man. Angus still wore last night's shapeless clothes, and his mass of hair almost stood on end. Perhaps that hair gave him the wild, untamed look so many women loved.

But the jaw. How often Harry had mentioned men coming to him to replicate a jaw like that? And Harry trying and failing. Here was the real thing. And yes, now she understood why so many males were willing to pay big bucks for that look.

"Miss Clearbell …"

Oh, the other men must have told Angus her name.

"… our phone's still not working, but I can take you where you want to go."

"Really?" She jumped up so fast she knocked her chair to the floor.

"Yes, I—"

She turned to lift the chair.

Four men struggled out the kitchen door to fight for the chair and push the old wooden thing upright.

"Well, thank you. I—"

Angus scowled. "Never mind the chair. As I was saying, I can take you to Inverness."

"Oh, thank you. I'm happy to pay."

A questioning look flitted across that rugged face as if payment had never been considered. My, he had beautiful eyes that switched from melting caramel to hot chocolate in a flash.

"Oh, yes, of course. Pay for the petrol."

"And for your time."

He scratched his head. "I head for Inverness now and again. I'll do some business while I'm there, so no need to pay for anything."

"Are you certain? I'm happy to pay."

"I think you'll need your money. I doubt you'll see your luggage again."

"But the bus driver said—"

"Probably didn't want to worry you. Aberdeen's some forty miles away. No one's going to travel that far on these roads to return your suitcase. Even if they wanted to."

"Oh." She slipped back down on the chair.

"I'm sure you can buy whatever you need in Inverness."

"Do they have a bridal shop?"

Angus' eyes changed from hot chocolate to nutty chestnut. His mouth widened into what she would call a relieved grin. "You're getting married!"

Not a question. A happy pronouncement. Well, that made both of them. She couldn't wait to see Harry … and become his bride. "Yes. It's leap year. I plan to ask him to marry me."

Angus' mouth dropped.

She'd never seen a handsome man look so gob-smacked.

"That's the dumbest thing I've ever heard."

The four men surrounding the table emitted loud murmurs so thickly Scottish she couldn't understand a word.

"Gonna no' dae that."

"Ye raff yer heid."

"Mad wae it."

"Awa' an bile ye rheid."

Heat flooded Charm's face. Angus was a jerk. She brushed hair back from her hot face. Evidently these other four sexist Scots didn't believe in leap year either.

What if Harry didn't? But he was American. And he loved her. Surely, he would accept her proposal.

What did she care what these strangers thought?

Flurry knew Harry.

And Harry was worth fighting for.

She just had to get to him.

Quickly.

CHAPTER 5

"Well, they say *love is blind*." Rick strode to the dining room window. With his back to Charm, he barked, "I'll be ready to head to Inverness in half an hour. Soon enough for you?"

She was going to ask some brainless fool to marry *her*? With her looks, what hot-blooded male could be crazy enough not to fly from Inverness to her home in America, break down her door, and carry her off to his man-cave? He'd have to be deaf not to rush to her melodious summons. Out of his mind not to see her potential as a wife and mother. Hard core not to melt under the magic of her presence. Unless …

Was she super intent on her career? What did she do to make enough money to race across the Atlantic to find some cretin living in Inverness without enough mental facilities to ask her to marry him? Was she a career-a-holic? No … she *wanted* to get married. But maybe she was a seductive-psycho-serial-husband-slayer?

Didn't look like one … but travelling in the storm to end all storms … hiring a broken-down bus driven by old Graeme who everyone knew wasn't rocking on all his skates. And spending the night in a diner. Rick rushed to the kitchen, jerked open the door, primed the water pump, filled a dishpan full, and plunged his head into the cool wetness. He had to give her that one. There *was no other* place to find shelter here in Fraserburgh.

He worked up a lather with the hand soap, washed his hair and face, and picked up his shaving cream. After she came back downstairs, he'd run up and grab a clean shirt and pants. They'd hop into the Smart Car and be on their way. A few hours driving *Brainiac,* and she'd be someone else's problem. A memory in his past. He shook his head. He was crazy not to fly the helicopter, but he wasn't in that much hurry to see her leave. He wasn't made of stone. She was a stunning woman.

Rick stretched his neck and ran the razor up his throat. There'd been a time when he would have thrust on full throttle and chased after this chick. He would have blasted on all engines without regard to the downwash and not stopped until he made her his.

"Ouch." He dabbed the nick in his neck. When was the last time he'd notched his throat? Couldn't remember. What could be wrong with the woman that she had to chase her man down and ask *him* to marry her? Certainly nothing on the lady's exterior would warn a man away. Had to be a personality problem. Crazy? Possibly. Pregnant? Hah. Nope. Any man would step forward and claim a child of hers and make his title legal.

Maybe she spent money like it cost no more than the air she breathed? From the looks of her clothes and shoes that *could be* a problem. He was no expert, but her clothes probably cost a bundle—before the storm botched them. He grinned. Although he enjoyed the shrunken look.

Maybe she nagged? Was a motor mouth? A criminal? A killer? A high maintenance diva?

But the four Aces, as he called the Scots who watched over the diner while he was away, seemed entranced with the lady. They hadn't found any glaring mysteries. Maybe she *was* a storm sorceress sent to seduce him. Kathleen might conjure up just such a person. He rinsed away the shaving cream fragments. No. Kathleen wouldn't have sent competition. Miss Clearbell would completely overshadow Kathleen, despite all her manipulations. And Kathleen expected his full attention.

So, what *was* wrong with Charm? A strange pang bit his chest as he buttoned his clean shirt. Sad, he'd never find out. Three hours tops, and Charm was out of his life.

If only he could say the same for Kathleen.

~

Charm stood at the bottom of the stairs.

Dougal hauled her overnight bag down the steep flight. "Doona let anyone nick yer case." He trudged out the front door, dragging her luggage behind him.

Fergus held her raincoat.

Duncan pressed a paper bag into her hands. "Lunch, Miss. Ye'll need a wee snack on the road. Ye'll be in Inverness before noon for sure and certain. Still, ye might like the snack before ye arrive."

She smiled. "Thank you."

Dougal stood by the open door, his hat in his hand. "Good travels, Miss.

She moved outside to the stone doorstep. "It has been a pleasure meeting all of you."

The gravel crunched, and she pivoted to see the car. "Oh no!"

"Aye, Miss. Angus be frugal with his money."

A red Smart Car stopped at the end of the unpaved lane, and Angus jumped out. He strode up the pathway to her and, as if he were in a great hurry, took the handle of her overnight bag from Dougal. He spoke to the middle button of his shirt as he smoothed the blue and white stripes with his free hand, "If you're ready, we'll be on our way."

The sun flitted from behind a cloud, and he stood tall and strong in its beaming rays.

She sucked in a breath. Whoa. Angus was such a hottie. A buffo. She could make a calendar just of him. Twelve months. Twelve outfits. Twelve ways to showcase his masculine perfection. Sexy seeped from his pores. What a difference light and a change of clothes made. He was definitely chiseled. And he had that strong, take-charge thing going on.

Harry. She needed to think about Harry. But right now, she wasn't in the right headspace for that. Couldn't even conjure a picture of him in her mind.

"Gie it laldy. I'm fair puckled." Dougal touched her arm.

She started. Oh, had she been staring? Standing by the car with her mouth wide open? She snapped her mouth shut and rounded the car to find Seumas holding the small car door wide open for her. But she couldn't force her gaze from Angus.

The man heaved her overnight to the top of the little car and proceeded to strap it down.

Suddenly alert, she rounded the front of the tiny car. "Oh, do make certain my case won't fall off. I need every item inside."

"Of course, you do." He cinched the strap tighter, so the car groaned. "I've got this. You get inside and find a place to stow that huge bag you call a purse. As you can see, there's no back seat."

He was in a mood this morning. Obviously, the handsome outside appearance didn't reflect the inner workings of the man. Mr. Grouch was back. Charm nodded. She could handle sourpuss, but could she handle Mr. Movie-star-testosterone-exuding-handsome? For the next three hours she'd settle for Mr. Annoying.

She crouched, bent further, and slid into the curved seat. Surprisingly comfortable. That is until she hauled her purse inside and clutched the shoulder bag on her lap. She lifted her rear from the seat and tried to smooth her dress lower over her legs, but the shrunken material stubbornly halted just below mid-thigh. She might as well have been wearing shorts. Actually, shorts would have been more comfortable. She should have worn her Yoga pants this morning. But she planned to stop at a dress store, and the dress had seemed more appropriate. Too late to change. Her case was strapped to the top of the car. Car? More like a glorified baby buggy.

The driver's side door opened. Angus slid into his seat with the ease of an acrobat. But his wide shoulders overflowed his seat and splayed over into her space.

"Ready?" He sat so close, warmth radiated from his body.

Welcome after the chill morning air, but she wound her arms around her shoulder bag and pressed herself against the passenger door. "Absolutely."

"Strapped in?"

"Tight."

"Okay, then." He started the car and slid smoothly onto the narrow road.

The bumps began. Felt as if the Smart Car had developed a dumb streak and sought out every bump and ridge in the rough road.

Between the irresistible presence and the ruts in the road, could she survive this trip intact?

~

Rick clutched the steering wheel with a grip of steel. Taking the Smart Car instead of the helicopter was a bad idea. Really, really bad. What was he thinking?

He glanced down to make certain she had latched her seat belt. Legs. Beautiful legs that went on forever. He was a sucker for shapely legs. And she smelled good. Had she brought her own soap in that big bag bouncing on the roof? She was slick and sophisticated ... or would have been if her dress hadn't been squashed through the wringer in the tail end of that hurricane. She was a rock star among all the girls he'd dated. Kathleen would be green. That would be bad. Would make that situation so much worse. For now, even though every clicking clacking cell in his brain screamed *no*, the *Brainiac* turned her wheels in the direction of Inverness.

He was insane thinking about the woman. But when someone this unbelievable dropped into his lap, he had to wonder why. Was God giving him a second chance? If so, why now, when he was so tangled up in this mess with Kathleen? Meeting Charm couldn't have happened at a worse time.

But wasn't that just like God? Faith without sight. He closed his eyes. *Lord, what should I do about Kathleen?*

"Look out!"

He swerved and ran off the road. Another twist of his wrist and *Brainiac's* short wheelbase had them back on the dirt road.

"Did you not see that animal?"

"Your scream distracted me."

"Ha! My scream distracted you from driving down this long, winding, empty road? Perhaps you should let me drive." She reached over to touch the wheel.

He snagged her wrist. "Not so fast. I get to drive because I'm big and strong and you're ... you know."

"I'm what?"

"Not as big or as strong."

"I'm more observant." She smiled.

"Since when?"

"Since we met."

"Give me an example." His mouth tilted up at the corners.

"You didn't see that animal and almost killed the poor thing."

"Ridiculous. I didn't hit the badger."

"You must be blind not to have seen that cute animal."

"I could drive this road blind."

"Not if an animal darts out. What if the animal had been a bear? And you hit a large hairy bear?" Her eyes grew big, and she slapped a hand over her mouth.

"We have no bears in this area. I'm alert and more than capable of driving. Do you have a Scottish license?"

"No." She made an elaborate gesture of checking her seatbelt and then settled back against the upholstery.

He focused on the empty, narrow road ahead. But his peripheral vision was too good. Always a plus for a pilot, but in this small space, nothing about her missed his retina. Okay. Three hours to make her change her mind. Three hours to have her so close. In this cool weather, he was sweating. Three hours to fight against thinking how much he'd like to kiss those tempting lips. Love at first sight. He needed a break. That just didn't happen.

What kind of guy could resist her? Why would he want to? His hand spasmed on the steering wheel. After one look at her last night, he'd been a goner. Way too late now to save his heart. Was the risk of falling for her worth the price he'd pay? Too late. Way too late. He'd fallen so deep so fast he'd never had a chance. Blind-sided. Like he was drunk. Tipsy in love.

This time he prayed with his eyes wide-open. *Lord, I don't understand why this woman showed up at this complicated time. But I've got to trust this meeting is from You. Don't let me mess up this time.*

He swerved and almost ran off the road. Again. What the heck?

Charm gasped. "Is the road this bad all the way to Inverness? You really should let me drive."

"No. Road gets smoother. Settle back. Relax. I'll get you to your destination safe and sound."

He'd get her there, but ... but? Okay, he didn't want to see her get hurt. What Neanderthal made a lady like Charm hunt him down like a hound after a fox. Nope, he'd set her straight.

He steered around a deep rut. "You can call me Rick. My friends call me Rick."

"Aren't Seumas, Dougal, Duncan, and Fergus your friends? And why Rick?"

"Angus Brode**rick** McDougal's my name. In Scotland everyone calls me Angus. Respect for my father, I think."

"Oh."

She was quiet for a beat, then— "Who calls you Rick?'

He sighed, deep and hard. "Long story. Sure, you want to know?"

"We have three hours."

"We could talk about you instead."

"Who calls you Rick?"

"Have it your way. I was born in Scotland. When I turned two, my parents moved to New York. I have dual citizenship."

She giggled. "That's your long story? So, that explains your lack of Scottish burr." Her laugh bubbled out. "Now you live part-time in New

York?"

"No. I live full-time in America. I came back this month to settle Dad's estate. He left the Fraserburgh Diner to me." He wiggled the car through a series of ruts with a minimum of bumps.

"Oh, I'm so sorry your father died."

"Yeah. I miss him. A lot."

"Did your father return to Scotland while you lived in New York?"

"Nope, Dad didn't come back here until a few weeks before he died. He had a bad heart and knew the end was coming. So, he returned to his childhood home to relive happy memories. His Dad was a fisherman by trade and also owned and ran the diner. I understand that back then the diner was *the* place to gather for an evening to eat a fine meal and converse with friends. Rather like a pub in Ireland."

She nodded. "From what I saw of the village, there wasn't much else available."

"True. However, Dad was devastated at the state of the inn and desired above all else to renovate the place and return the diner to its former glory."

"So now the Fraserburgh Inn is yours."

"It is."

"And all the villagers are anxious that you stay and renovate the historic building?"

"That's the size of it."

"And?"

"I'm not even torn. I have a job I love back in the States. I'm putting the Fraserburgh up for sale as soon as I get home."

"New York?"

"Umm."

"Today?"

"Umm."

"You're not going back to the diner today?"

"I have business in Inverness. Don't know how long that will take."

"Do you have time to drop me at a bridal shop?"

Rick swallowed. Cleared his throat. *Lord, You're nudging her my way.* "Kathleen's Bridal Shop is a short detour. It's in Bridgend. But you can also purchase street clothes there too. I doubt you want to approach your boyfriend wearing …" He waved at her dress.

"How observant of you."

"That's me. I see every critter crossing the road." He ran his fingers through his hair. Today was Kathleen's day off at the bridal shop. Dare he risk the slight chance she might stop in?

"How short a detour?"

"About an hour."

"Is that the only bridal shop?"

"Only one I know."

"Fine. Let's go there first, then."

Rick pulled in a deep breath. That gave him an extra two hours with the woman of his dreams. His once-in-a-lifetime woman. If she ever found out he could have flown her to Inverness in about thirty minutes … man, was he sticking his neck out on a limb. He barely braked as he took the turn-off to Bridgend.

ANNE GREENE

CHAPTER 6

Rick reached across and patted her seatbelt. "Good thing you're belted in."

Charm nodded and smiled. "How sweet of you to take the extra time I need to shop. I hope the delay won't inconvenience you."

"Not at all. My business in Inverness is not time sensitive. Happy to help."

"So, what do you do in New York?"

"I moved from New York a number of years ago."

"Oh. Where do you live?"

He grinned. "Tampa."

"Not really! *You* live in Tampa?" She twisted in her seat and pointed her thumb at her chest. "I live in Tampa."

Was she surprised happy? Or surprised as if he were just another stranger she might run into from time to time? Or didn't give a hoot? Her big blue eyes sparked, and her beautiful smile seemed genuine as if he were someone she'd like to meet on a regular basis. Sweat popped onto his forehead. A man would die to keep that smile on her face.

Gravel crunched as the right tires caught on the outer rim of the road. He switched his attention from her magnetizing presence to his driving, flicked his wrist, and steered Brainiac back on the road.

She didn't seem to notice.

"I can't believe I travel all the way to Scotland and meet someone who lives in Tampa. What are the odds?"

Yeah, God. What's going on here? "Small world." Blast. Now she'll want to know what he did for a living.

She shifted her big purse on her lap. "I live in an apartment on Harbour Island with my best friend and roomie, Flurry Foster. We're both Corporate Travel Agents."

"Sounds like an interesting job."

"Yes. But I don't get to travel nearly as much as I'd like. Mostly I work online with my clients and only visit the places they want to go when I have a large contract and need to scope out the setting and set up their reservations in person."

"But here you are in Scotland tagging after a man who doesn't have enough sense to ask you to marry him." Blast, he didn't usually have a problem keeping a lid on his mouth."

"Well, Harry is unaware this *is* leap year."

Rick shook his head. That kind of thinking rattled his brain. "If you need to ask him to marry you, he's just not that into you."

Her face crumbled. "You're certainly opinionated."

Blast his tongue. He rounded a curve too fast, and the wheels screeched. Well, she needed to know. Best to get that information out in the open.

"You're not a very nice person."

He put on a scowl. Probably be good if she continued thinking that way. He fixed his stare on the road.

~

Charm shrugged. The man was so gorgeous on the outside, but inside he was cruel. How would Rick have the slightest idea if Harry wanted to marry her or not? Harry only needed to be reminded that time was passing. Precious days when they could better be starting their family. She really wanted four beautiful children. Regardless of what college professors preached, raising a family was still what God desired for His children. Be fruitful and multiply. He had ordered. Her college professors didn't believe in God, and so they taught students to enjoy their lives, travel, amuse themselves, and do what pleased them. They preached families were a burden and an expense. Finding oneself and self-expression was the fulfilling way to live. Balderdash.

She didn't fall for that propaganda. A woman was born to have, love, and nourish children. Anything else she did placed the cherry on top of the sundae. True, careers fulfilled but didn't comfort one in her old age. She believed in the old-fashioned way. Children first, then career or a balance of the two. And she would celebrate with twenty-seven candles on her cake in December. Time for Harry to step-up and move things along.

Sure, she loved her career—but she could slip away from agenting for a few years and once her children were in school slide right back into place.

Many of the ladies she knew had done just that.

Harry was the only hitch to her plan. He admitted he wanted kids, but not yet. His career was in full swing, and he loved his life. Just. As. It. Was. And she loved Harry.

Fluttering in her stomach made it ache. A headache nagged her. She did love Harry, didn't she? She hugged her purse to her chest. Of course, she did. Just because she sat so close to a man who radiated masculine pheromones simply by his proximity didn't mean she didn't love Harry. Besides, Rick was not a nice person. Certainly not a gentleman.

Okay, too late for a comeback. He had to have seen how his comment devastated her. But she wouldn't pout here silently like a peeved child. "So, where in Tampa do you live?"

Rick steered the Smart Car around a particularly large hole in the pavement. "I live on Davis Island. Near the Peter O Knight Airport."

"Ha! We must only live a few miles from one another. Imagine that."

"Yeah."

Hmm. He didn't seem inclined to talk. That brooding expression would have been off-putting on someone else, but on Rick the look was somehow endearing. How could such an insufferable man look endearing? "And what is your line of work?"

He winced. Actually winced.

"Umm, we should be coming up soon to Bridgend. Do you know what you want to buy?"

"Oh yes. I'll try on wedding gowns, of course. And then I'll need several dresses for evening, and some for daytime wear. I don't suppose you know what ladies in Inverness wear. Are they fashion conscious or more country types? I don't want to stand out as a stranger."

He glanced at her. "I don't think you need worry about standing out. There's never a place you won't stand out."

What did that mean? He didn't even have to try to be contrary. "I mean are the ladies more big-jewelry-Miami or big-casual-Tampa."

"I don't have a clue what you mean."

"Do they dress to the nines or are they casual?"

"I'm afraid I'm not much help in the what-do-women-wear department."

"Okay, when you take your girl on a date, does she go in a dress or in jeans?"

"I'd guess dress."

"Okay, that's helpful." Men, they were so useless in some departments.

He went back to brooding.

She started tapping her foot. "So, you live near the airport, do you go to the dog park? I have a Shih Tzu and take her to the dog park at least once every two weeks."

"Nope, no dog."

"I'm guessing from the way you drive this car that you're not a bus driver."

He laughed. Actually threw back his head and guffawed. "No, you're right, not a bus driver."

"What do you do that you love your job so much you don't want to move to Scotland and take over that charming diner?"

"I'm a pilot."

Wow, considering the way he drove, that was unexpected. "What airline?"

"Air Medical Transport Service. I fly helicopters called air ambulances from the scene of an injury or accident to and from hospitals for critical care and emergency flights."

Charm pulled in a breath. "Really?" She relaxed against the car cushions. "That's impressive. I understand why you love your job."

"Yeah. I fly for Tampa General Hospital and fly as far as Clearwater and Sarasota. I know the air over the coast of Florida like the back of my hand." His face glowed.

"How long have you been in Fraserburgh?"

"A little over two weeks."

"So, you don't really know these local roads or the exact way to Inverness?"

"I've got my GPS."

"Did you notice a few miles back how this road narrowed, and the pavement grew more potted with holes?"

Red tinged Rick's cheeks. "If you think we're lost—no. Think again."

Just ahead a barricade spanned the road that had turned into a weedy lane.

He put the car in reverse, and the wheels spun, then dug into the mud, and sat still.

Kaput.

CHAPTER 7

"Who needs a roller coaster when they can ride with you? I wasn't looking for adventure, but I found it anyway with your crazy driving." Charm unfastened her seat belt.

Rick had one leg out the door and twisted back to stare at her. "You stay put. The road's—"

Too late. Charm peered down at her strappy heeled shoe squashed almost to her ankle with gooey mud. "I was planning to help push."

Rick was out of the car like a hurdle jumper and over at her side.

She tried pulling her foot out of the muck, but the poor overworked skinny strap across her arch broke. She lifted her oozing bare foot, her black heel slowly burying itself in the thick ooze. "Oh, no."

Rick bent and rescued her shoe. "Now this is one practical mud boot." He tried flicking sludge from the mess, but only managed to clean a portion—enough to show the shoe was beyond saving. "Hope you weren't planning on wearing this again." He glanced down at his own shoes perched on a dryer portion of the road, but soles still covered with black slush. He handed her the ruined high heeled shoe. "Please don't get out. I'll push us out of this gunk."

She craned her neck to watch him move to the rear of the stuck car.

Rick slipped and fell flat on his back.

Charm doubled over in laughter.

Rick struggled to stand, sloughing off the mud, and shook like a dog. Clods of mud splattered on the wet grass and squashy trail. He laughed. "Thanks for asking, but no, I'm not hurt. Just my pride."

She stuffed her hand over her mouth and tried to stop giggling.

"Glad *you're* having fun with this." He walked uphill to a heavy patch of grass and dropped flat to roll on his backside and dislodge as much mud as he could. He called, "Road's too muddy. We'll have to wait until the pavement dries out some before I push Brainiac from the pothole." He jumped up, did a shimmy.

She bent doubt with laughter. "Is that a Scotch saber dance?"

He smiled. "Just a little something to keep your spirits up." He stepped down from the hill, rounded the car to her window and leaned down. "Shouldn't take more than an hour or two before the mud dries enough for me to push."

Her throat tightened. "And in the meantime?"

Rick straightened, scratched his head, and gazed around. It's pretty dry out here above the road. Looks like there's a coffee shop or café at the top of the hill. We could go up there and wait. What do you say?"

As if his words brightened a dull world, the sun suddenly burst out in a warm display of beauty, transforming the surroundings into a clean, fresh, green world.

Charm pulled in a deep exhilarating breath and smiled. At last, the sun! She opened her door. Could she jump across the quagmire of mud between her and the dry land? And what of her shoe?

Suddenly, Rick leaned down, cradled her in his arms and lifted her from the car seat. He pivoted and began to ascend the steep hill, still hugging her in his embrace. One bare foot dangled and the other still shod foot draped over his arms.

"You can't carry me all the way to the café!"

"Watch me."

He wasn't even breathing hard.

She was pressed between the hard muscles of his arms and his chest … and the sensation of her body against his was delightful. She relaxed.

But surely, she was too heavy a burden for him to carry to the top of the hill.

His breathing increased.

"No, you must let me walk. This is too much a strain for you."

"And the ground is too hard and prickly with thistles for you to walk. Lie still. We're almost at the top."

He was huffing now.

Well, he *was* the one who got the car stuck. She rested her forehead against his stubborn chin.

But his face was red and sweat beaded his forehead. She mustn't give him a heart attack. "Please I can walk from here."

"Almost … to … the … top."

My, the man was obstinate. But so sweet to carry her. And she was so enjoying the ride.

The second his shoes reached level ground he swung her to her feet. "There, you can walk here." Sweat poured down his forehead like a burst waterpipe. He swiped the wet with his sleeve and blinked. "Salt's burning my eyes."

"Let me help." She grabbed a tissue from her purse and dabbed his face. Paused and caught her breath. What nice eyes he had. Large and brown with gold flecks. She tilted her head. Narrowed her eyes in thought. *Now, what color are Harry's?* What a puzzle. Of course, she knew the shape and color and expression of Harry's eyes. Just now she couldn't bring them to mind.

Rick turned his head.

Broke her concentration. Had she been staring again? He must think her a country bumkin.

The cords in his neck throbbed. "Looks like the place is open for business. Am I unmuddied enough to go inside?"

"Passably." Her own pulse raced. His from exertion—hers from excitement. She gazed at the quaint building in front of them. Inviting … but … Had Harry's mere presence ever raised her pulse? But then, Harry had never carried her … anywhere. She shook her head and thrust her shoulders back. No, Harry had never put her in a position where he had to tote her around like a sack of sweet potatoes. He was much more sensible.

But much less exciting.

She gave herself a mental slap. "Let's go

inside. I need a drink of water."

She picked her way up the sandy path to the front door. He took her elbow to help as she hobbled on one bare foot and one high heeled shoe.

The café had appeared quaint from a distance, but now showed itself to be seedy and in great need of repair. The door hung lopsided from a broken hinge.

"Appears this place has seen better days. Probably was prosperous before the powers that be put the highway in." Rick pulled the door open. The hinges screeched like a braying jackass.

"The highway you turned off of a number of miles back?"

"Yep. That's the one."

Inside the small room was dim with a band of sunshine trying hard to beam inside through the dirty windowpane. "Looks like the window hasn't been washed since King Arthur stayed here." Three dusty tables surrounded by sad-looking chairs hunkered next to an empty windowed counter that had probably at one time been filled with pastries.

"You got that right." Using his hand, Rick dusted one of the chairs. "You can sit while I scout the place to see if I can find us some water to drink."

"You're the one who climbed the hill. You sit while I search for water."

"But you're barefoot. You might walk on a nail or get splinters in your foot. I'm fine. I'll see what this place has to offer."

"I think I can walk around without stubbing my toe. While you might keel over from exhaustion."

An exasperated look crossed Rick's face. "Have it your way. We'll both look for water." He stomped toward the far end of the room.

Glancing at the uneven floorboards, hairy spiders came to mind. Yuck. She slid down onto the chair Rick had dusted. Perhaps this time he was right.

~

Rick shuffled off, eyes taking in the dirt, the desolation, and the loneliness of the forsaken café. Maybe that Harry of hers had a point. Charm was nothing if not obstinate. Maybe Harry didn't want Charm running his life, and that's why the man proved so hard to get.

Rick wiped his sweaty forehead with his sleeve. He'd about busted a gut carrying her up here. Dumb thing to do. But the idea of sitting in Brainiac for a couple hours waiting for the sun to dry the mud hole had been too much. Being so close to the dazzling girl would have driven him over the edge of his resistance.

He grunted. Only to find he was still alone with her. No groups of happy people eating and drinking to take his thoughts off Charm even for an instant. Nope. Still alone with her. And now he knew the feel of her. He raked his hand through his hair. Nope. Don't go there. She was taken. In love with another man. Off limits. Not for him.

Unless …

That was his plan, wasn't it? The one he hadn't thought through. The one he'd gone off on, half-loopy with the thought of her marrying another man. This was not him. This was some out of his mind, misguided stranger who had taken over his heart.

He was a solid man who knew his own mind, who set his course, and made the future happen the way he carefully planned in advance. He was a man who piloted helicopters, drove cars without accidents, sold the diner, and returned to Tampa to his responsible job and no-nonsense home.

That was him. He made a beeline to the water pump. On the way picked up two dingy glasses. Then used his excessive energy working the pump as if the house was on fire. Then he rinsed his hands completely clean and filled two glasses of water.

But he was also the guy who got tangled in Kathleen's net and hadn't found a way out. Since that first and only date, he'd avoided Kathleen like the plague.

Now he was the guy who'd fallen hopelessly head over heels, crazy-minded, win her or die, in love with Charm.

No way was he himself.

CHAPTER 8

Charm perched on one of the chairs Rick
had brought from inside the deserted café and
placed on the stone patio. She gazed down the steep
hill to a luxuriously green panorama. The world
looked washed clean, and the fresh scent intoxicated
her. "If a person must be stranded, this is the perfect
spot."

Rolling hills undulated lazily until they
reached a delightfully quaint-looking village a mile
or so away. Stone houses clustered around an
ancient church whose spire rose toward heaven. Off
to the side, pastures enclosed with rail fences held
tiny specs of white that she could just discern were
herds of sheep. Two sheep dogs circled the flock
and ushered them through an open gate. The tiny
form of a man trailed after the animals.

"Oh, this is so tranquil, so beautiful. I'm almost
glad your Brainiac got stuck." She laughed. "Do
you suppose she got her wheels mired on purpose to
give us this fun adventure?" She giggled. "Of
course, she didn't."

Rick threw back his head and laughed so hard
his chair tipped to one side, and he almost slid off.
He righted himself. "You're liking this wee trip, are

ye?" He spoke with a thick, Scottish accent that sounded phony as a bald man's toupee.

"Aye, very much." Charm tossed her long hair back over her shoulder and blessed Rick with her warmest smile. She pointed to the village. "Is that Bridge End?"

He nodded. "If my GPS is correct, that is Bridge End."

"Have you never been there?"

Red tinged his lean cheeks. A tic rippled in his set jaw. "Once, but I approached from Inverness, not Fraserburg."

She cocked her head. "Something happened in Bridge End? Let me guess, you got a traffic ticket for going over twenty through town."

"Ha, nothing so simple."

"You were arrested for trying to kidnap the Loch Ness monster?"

"Ha. Wrong part of Scotland."

"I've got it. Something with a woman?"

A frown flashed across his forehead which he quickly erased. "You're a curious lady, Charm."

The way he spoke her name sent currents of delight skinning up and down her spine. "Well, curiosity is killing this feline. Tell me."

Instead, Rick pushed against the chair with his long legs until he balanced on the back two legs. He began humming.

She joined in as together they sang – "'Ye'll take the high road, and I'll take the low road, and I'll be in Scotland afore ye … For me and my true love will never meet again, on the bonnie, bonnie banks of Loch Lomond.'"

She stopped singing. "What do you suppose that song means?"

Rick cleared his throat. "Here's one interpretation of the lyrics. Celtic culture believed that fairies return the souls of the deceased to their homeland. Back in the spring of 1746, after the disastrous Scottish loss at the Battle of Culloden, many men on the losing side, Scottish Jacobite ringleaders, were arrested and taken for trial in faraway London where they knew they would be hanged. In some cases, accused pairs were given a choice. One would die, and the other would live. The song is a bittersweet reassurance, sung from the one who chose death to the survivor. The soon to be deceased would take the spiritual *low road* to be united with his Scottish homeland where his soul will be reunited with the living who will return on the spiritual *high road* which is over land."

Charm swallowed. "Oh, that's so sad. Perhaps that's why the song resounds with so many people."

"Possible." Rick spread out with his arms high and his hands behind his head.

Her heart sped. He looked so relaxed, so approachable, so very personable. Not at all did he resemble the Fraserburg Diner's owner. After all, he *had* taken her in when she had no place else to go. He *had* given her his own room when there was no other. He *had* taken his time to drive her to buy her wedding dress, and he would take her to the arms of her soon-to-be fiancé. He really was quite a lovely man. If she were not about to be engaged …. She shook her head.

His eyes were closed, and his face lifted to the

sun. He had that magnificent jaw line, and his nose was not too narrow, not too broad, but actually just right for his face. And his lips ... oh she really shouldn't look at those really interesting ... actually enticing lips. What would kissing him be like?

There was a smudge of mud just above his left eyebrow. She lifted her hand. No, she would not allow herself to brush that slender line of dried earth from his brow. She was a woman about to become engaged.

"So, what type of music do you like?" His eyes remained closed, but a smile turned his lips up at the corners.

She thought for a second. What did she like? "Oh, anything I can sing to. Hum to. Clap to. Dance to. I like the whole range of music from choir anthems to 50s jitterbug, to country to classical."

"Nice. And what does that leap-year man of yours like?"

"Harry likes ... I'm not sure. I don't think we've ever gotten around to talking music."

Rick sprang up so fast his chair slid in the drying grass. He caught his balance and gazed into her eyes. "Does he know your favorite color? What you like to eat? Where you like to spend your time? What your dreams are?" He turned away and gazed down at the distant village. "Does he know how many children you want? Does he care what church you attend? What does this Harry guy know about you?"

Charm blinked. Where had all that fervor come from? "I think Harry knows a lot about me. We've been dating a year now. He knows I like mixed flowers with a heavy emphasis on pink Star Gazers." She frowned. Then why did he always bring red roses? "He knows I like to eat at one favorite restaurant as opposed to trying new places." Then why did Harry avoid taking her to *Our Place By The Sea* in Tampa? He'd taken her there once months ago. But as soon as he learned the legend, he'd avoided returning.

"So, what is *your* favorite restaurant in Tampa?" The words came slow and languid from his interesting lips.

"I love *Our Place By The Sea*. Do you know it?

"I thought that was a cemetery."

She punched his arm. "Oh, stop teasing!"

"Yeah, I've heard of that one. The restaurant's on Harbour Island, right?"

"Yes." She couldn't help but smile.

"Isn't there a legend that goes with the place, or do I have that one mixed with another? Doesn't the fable go something like—if you meet a person of the opposite sex for the first time at *Our Place By The Sea,* you'll fall in love with that person for life."

"Yes." Charm giggled. "You believe that legend, but don't believe in Leap Year?"

"I didn't say I believed that fairy tale. I said I heard the story." Rick gave a crooked grin. "I'm willing to bet you didn't meet Prince Charming, Harry at *Our Place By The Sea.*

She'd been feeling so happy and light, but a flash of remembrance burst her bubble. "Um, you're right. My boss had set up a blind date for us." She rubbed her chin. "We, ah. Harry and I were supposed to meet at *Our Place*. But at the last moment Harry called me and suggested we meet at his country club instead. I think he mentioned something about being allergic to fish."

"So, is he?"

"Harry never mentioned a fish allergy again." But they had eaten crab together several times. And she'd only talked Harry into taking her there one time. He said he didn't like the ambiance. She'd never puzzled that one out. *Our Place* was such a delightful spot.

"So, old Harry avoided that place as if it was jammed with chains and a prison door. Didn't that give you a clue?"

"That's just one restaurant in hundreds. And he doesn't like fish." She *had* wondered. Then forgotten. Their romance had been such a whirl-wind. Parties, restaurants, outings, sailing, movies, friends, seldom alone. She rubbed the nape of her neck. What did she really know of Harry? Glamor and excitement. They'd seldom spent much time alone. He had an insatiable desire for activity. And to be surrounded by people.

"Earth to Charm. "

"I'm sorry. I got lost in thought."

He glanced around the quiet countryside. "Good place to think."

No. Not when her thoughts were negative. She needed to think happy before she purchased her wedding gown. She would only marry once, and she intended to make sure she was asking the right man. "I still can't believe you live in Tampa. How strange to meet you here."

Rick winked with all the seduction of an enchanter. "Maybe meeting me was God's plan for your life. Our lives are too busy in Tampa so He brought us here so we could encounter one another."

Rick's words made goosebumps slide down her arms. "Wow, now that's a theory." Charm shook her head. "Only problem is, He brought me here to Scotland to propose to my boyfriend."

"And yet, you haven't found that elusive guy, have you? So, where's Seymour?"

"His name is Harry. And no. I haven't found him, but I will. As soon as your silly little car is unstuck from the mud, we've only a short way to the bridal shop. That's right, isn't it?"

"Unless you change your mind."

"I didn't come all the way to Scotland to change my mind. I'll soon have my wedding dress, some clothes, and." She looked down at her one bare foot and one foot still tucked into her strappy high heels. "And some new shoes."

Rick glanced up at the sun. "Pretty hot. Maybe Brainiac's about to be unglued from her quagmire. Wait here, and I'll bring you another drink before we go down." He hopped up, pivoted, and reentered the café door. His footsteps thumped on the wooden floor, the back door screeched, then silence.

Dear Father God, did Rick actually suggest You might have orchestrated our meeting? Is he really interested in knowing me better? Or more, in dating me? Is he coming on to me? I don't know how to read him. She shook her head. Surely not. She'd made herself abundantly clear she'd come to

Scotland for one purpose. And she would marry Harry. So, what was Rick's game?

~

Rick stuck his head under the flowing water from the pump. What a chump. Blubberhead. Flake. He'd as much as confessed that he adored her. What was wrong with him? Telling her his thoughts almost before he thought them. Yes. It occurred to him that God brought them together in this strange, unlikely way. But he was nowhere near sharing that information with her. Seemed he'd been encircled by Wonder Woman's Truth Lasso. He had no control over what he said.

He shook his head, splashing water in great circles, then ran his fingers through his wet mat of hair. Okay, maybe his heart was right. If so, he didn't have the gift of time. The woman was going to propose to another man. She propose to that guy? So wrong. The man would accept. What man would not? Rick shook his head. So, he didn't have much time. He knew what he wanted. He would go after her like a wildfire in the Serengeti.

He held the two glasses under the lessening drip from the pump. But he didn't want to scare her off. Make her think he was some bumbling Casanova. All he had to do was prevent her from marrying this other guy, this Harry Bear ... then make her fall in love with him.

Simple, right?

And he only had a day or two at the most ... until she met this man of hers.

So, yes. Take off the brakes ... put the helicopter in gear ... hover over her until she fell for him … or not.

Whoa, he was headed for heartbreak hill. Wrong, he was climbing heartbreak hill.

But he had to give their relationship everything he had. Warp speed.

Thank God. Kathleen wasn't in her shop today.

CHAPTER 9

"Okay, hop aboard. The only way you're going to descend that steep hill is on my back." Rick's heart warmed. He loved that startled expression that made her eyes so large in her lovely face.

"Oh, no. I'm far too heavy for you. You looked wiped out after you carried me up here. I can't take advantage of you again." She began picking her way over the gravel, thistles, and grass toward the descent. "Ouch. Oh. Ugh." She looked up, her expression perplexed. "I'm so sorry. But it seems you are right. There's only one way down for me without lacerating my feet."

Rick grinned. She couldn't weigh more than 110-120 pounds. He could manage that. He moved over to stand in front of her and bent so she could grasp his shoulders. "Satisfying to have you agree with me."

"Don't let this victory go to your head." She hopped up, grasped his shoulders, and wound her legs around his waist.

Umm, having her so close made the blood surge through his body. But ... umph ... she seemed to weigh more this second time around. A healthy lady. He'd forgotten how tough going up the hill had been. Drained some of his strength. But now, descending, he had to watch his footing on loose rocks. Stupid, thinking the café was still in operation. Appeared that this lonely branch off the main road had been forsaken when the Scots put in the new highway. Highway was so recent it hadn't shown up on his GPS. So, he'd taken the old road.

"Am I too heavy?"

"Nope. Piece of cake." Big piece of cake.

"I think I'm putting you off-balance going downhill. We're top heavy."

"No worries. Relax and enjoy the ride."

Her cheerful answer floated down. "Tis a lovely ride."

He concentrated on keeping his footing and trying not to huff and puff. He'd have to hit the gym more often when he returned to Tampa. At least the ground had dried out enough so he no longer walked on a spongy surface.

He finally felt level ground beneath his feet. There she was. Brainiac waiting for them. Her four wheels deep in drying ruts. Shouldn't be any problem pushing her up on the slightly higher, now almost dry dirt road. They could be on their way. How does a man show a woman he loves her?

"You can let me down now. I can walk on the road." She did a little wiggle.

He bent backward, and she slid off.

He resisted rotating his shoulders and bending his back to relieve the cramps. Instead, he faced her. "You're no burden at all. I'm available anytime you need a ride … transportation …" He shook his head.

She could take his words any number of ways. "I mean, stand right here, and I'll push the car out of those ruts."

He jumped to Brainiac's rear, jammed both hands against her round rear end and shoved.

The car lurched, then sunk back into the rut. Oh, oh, this was harder than he expected.

Charm moved to his side. "On your three count, we'll push together." Hands on the car's rear, she bent beside him.

"One. Two. Three." They bulldozed together until Brainiac lurched out of the rut and onto smooth road.

She peeked at him a Cheshire Cat grin on her delightful face, her incredible blue eyes sparkling. "We work well together, don't you think?"

"Legendary. We are a team."

A blush tinted her lovely complexion. "Well, a team for a day."

"We could make the teamwork last a lifetime."

She raised her brows and shuttled to the passenger side, opened the door, and slid into the seat.

He pulled in a deep breath and shuffled to the driver's side. He took some more deep breaths, then slid behind the wheel. "Where's that lunch Duncan packed for us? We could eat, then be on our way."

Charm scrambled down by her feet and lifted the full paper bag. She delved inside and brought out two cellophane-wrapped sandwiches. "Peanut butter and jelly. My favorite." She handed him one.

Before he took his first bite, he asked, "What's your address in Tampa?"

She glanced sideways at him, a tiny smile making her lips even more enticing. "I don't usually tell men my address, but we've been through so much together, and you've been so over-the-top kind, I'll write it for you."

"I'd remember."

"You have some super memory that you recall the address of every damsel in distress you've helped?"

"You're not just a damsel in distress. You've become a great deal more to me these few days we've known one another."

"Oh well …." She rustled around in the lunch sack as if she could make enough noise to drown out his words. She came up with a scone and some jam. "Here's one for you. They look delicious."

"Should be. Duncan makes them from scratch. He's been acting chef since I returned."

She didn't look at him. Gazed out the window as if she'd never seen the landscape before. "Have you decided what you will do with your diner?"

"I'm going to deed the diner and the property to the four men you met. They and the town need a gathering place. I don't need a property in Scotland. Don't plan to return again unless I come for a vacation."

"Lovely and generous, but oh, can you afford not to sell the place to them?"

He crumpled the empty cellophane in his fist and took a bite of the scone. After he swallowed, he put a hand on her arm until she turned to face him. "I don't need the money, and the guys don't have the money. Since I don't want to move to Scotland,

I'm sure my dad would be happy to see his old friends take over the diner."

"But Scotland is lovely. You seem very much at home here."

"My job, my home," he gazed into her azure eye, "and my heart are in Tampa."

"Oh my," Charm glanced at her watch. "It's getting late. How long does the bridal shop stay open?"

"You're not really planning to go ahead with your cockamamie leap year plan, are you?"

"Of course. I've hit a speed bump in finding Harry, but my plan is still—"

He moved sideways, cradled his arms around her, pulled her close, and kissed those beguiling lips. Long and sweet.

She didn't resist. Kissed him back.

He was not nearly ready when she pulled away.

She finished her sentence. "On track. First a dress, then find Harry." She pushed against his chest.

Immediately he released her.

"And don't try to sabotage my plan."

Charm settled back into Brainiac's cushioned seat. If she hadn't been in love with Harry, she might think she was falling for Rick. But that idea was silly. She'd dated Harry over a year. And she'd only known Rick two days. The man couldn't possibly be in love with her.

Sure Rick was handsome and funny. Generous and so very helpful. And that kiss had blown her away. After that kiss, she couldn't even remember what or if or when she'd ever kissed Harry. Her brain was scrambled. She wasn't born yesterday. A man who could overwhelm her with excited pulse and answering lips had to know his way around women. Lots of women. A guy that seemed too good to be true … had to be.

CHAPTER 10

Rick's grip on the steering wheel tightened. Okay he overstepped. Fine line he had to walk. Didn't want to scare Charm off. He checked the GPS on his phone. Where did this ridiculous cow path intersect with the new main road? If he remembered correctly, the bridal shop closed early on Wednesday, but no way did he want Charm to know he'd gotten stuck in the mud on purpose to make them arrive too late for the woman he'd fallen for at first sight to purchase a wedding dress to marry Harry the Hidden.

None of his efforts had swayed her in her plan, but he had sure as the devil dug himself deeper in love. He could picture the two of them in Tampa, getting married in whatever venue she wanted, small and simple or elaborate and inclusive. A fantastic honeymoon in Bali where she'd never give the slippery Harry Bear a single thought, then moving together to a larger apartment ... or a house if that's what she wanted. He liked Harbour Island, close enough to the airport, but if her work was further away, they could move close to her job. Whatever she wanted.

"What company do you work for?"

She smiled. "Corporate Vacations International. I love helping companies award bonuses to deserving employees, or planning a Team Building Vacation, or even just serving the CEOs. Annual Meetings are fun as well. I've seen pictures of some of the most exotic places in the world. But I've only managed to visit a few. I do get a small discount on plane tickets, hotels, and car rentals, but my salary doesn't stretch far enough to do extensive travel." She giggled. "This little trip is costing me next to nothing so far. I love having ventured off the beaten track."

"Glad you like our glorious Scotland even though this time of year doesn't show her off at her best."

"I thought you'd only been here a short time?"

How he adored those lips parted in surprise. "I was here as a lad. But mostly my dad regaled me with stories and descriptions of places he loved. He could spin quite the yarn." *He would have delighted in meeting you. It pained him I never was interested in a girl enough to ask her to marry me.* A pang ripped through Rick's heart. "My dad would have liked you."

"Thank you."

"So, what about your parents? Where do they live? Do you have any siblings?"

"I have a best friend whom I love as my sister. Her name is Flurry Foster. She's also a Travel Agent at Corporate Vacations International. I have no siblings, and my dad died when I was a baby. I don't remember him at all. My mother went to her heavenly adventure four years ago."

"I'm so sorry. You have no relatives living near you? *Dear God, no wonder she wants to get married. She needs a rock in her life. And that cad, Harry, leaves her hanging.* "Cousins, aunts, uncles, grandparents?"

"Yes, I have cousins, aunts, uncles, but no grandparents. But my relatives all live in the Minot, North Dakota area. It's way too cold in the winter there for me, so I moved to Tampa about five years ago. I love that glorious city."

He took his hand off the wheel and laid it over hers. "I, for one, am delighted you moved from Minot to Tampa. I have Air Force friends, and they tell me chilling tales of that town. Tiny, built around the Air Force base there, but good people. Impossibly cold temperatures. Outside the air base and playing hockey, they do gather at churches and find friends there. Not much else in the area."

"Yep. That's Minot." She left her hand snug beneath his.

Brainiac bumped so hard she almost bounced off the road. And they were on the main highway.

He accelerated slightly on the paved road.

"We can go faster now, don't you think?" Charm leaned forward gazing out the front window.

He pressed harder on the gas. "We should arrive in just a few minutes."

A quaint church rose up on the right side. A bistro and sandwich shop began a line of interesting little shops filling both sides of the wide street. Groups of people strolled the sidewalks.

"This looks like a touristy kind of town. The shops are so quaint and picturesque. Just lovely."

Charm clasped her hands and gazed out the car window, her dimples playing hide and seek in her cheeks. "Oh, look." She pointed. "We're here. That sign reads *Kathrine's Bridal Boutique.* Oh, what a perfect shop." She turned to face him. "I can't thank you enough for bringing me here. I'm sure to find the perfect wedding dress." She bobbed up and down on the seat, her azure eyes full of wonder.

Rick choked and swallowed. When she found that horrible Harry, he would fall at her feet and marry her on the spot. Rick wiped at the sudden sweat beading his forehead. And he had to take her to buy her wedding dress. This was Dante's third level of Hell.

A car pulled out of a slot directly in front of Katherine's fancy door. He slipped into the spot and shut off the motor. *So, what now, God? She finds her perfect dress and her perfect fiancé, and they have the perfect wedding. What have I done to deserve this?*

Charm didn't wait for him. She flung herself out of the car, hobbled up the sidewalk, and slipped inside on one bare foot and one strappy heel.

Rick sighed. Counted to ten. Breathed deep. Should he go inside or wait out here? He rolled down the window. No breeze. Now the August sun felt too hot. Smothering. The little car held heat like a pizza oven.

He read the etching on the front door. *Open 9 to 5 six days a week. Welcome, Come On In. We have clothes for every occasion. This is a happy shop. If you want it, we've got it.*

No more up close and personal hugging or

caveman carrying the woman he loved. She'd have a complete pair of shoes. Able to walk on her own two feet. Plus, she'd have that white wedding gown. She'd look an angel. For someone else.

Maybe he'd go across the street and nurse a cup of coffee and his broken heart at the café until she finished her shopping.

He put his hand on the door handle.

The shop door opened, and Charm leaned out and beckoned. "Come inside. I need your opinion."

Huh. If he gave his opinion, he'd tell her to race to the airport and get on the first flight back to Tampa and forget hard-to-pin-down Harry. The man didn't deserve her.

He opened the door, thrust out a leg, and unfolded. His legs felt like dead sticks as he walked to the ornate door. Should have gone for that coffee.

~

Why was Rick dawdling so? Charm held the door open. "I really want your opinion. There are so many beautiful dresses to choose from. I've already found bridal shoes that are too stunning. And," She held up a pair of heels that had a few slender straps attached to the soles. "These are adorable, don't you think?"

Red tinged Rick's face as he walked inside. He looked around the dainty interior shop as if he were a lusty bull at a tea party.

She could imagine his chagrin. White carpet, spindly gold chairs, mirrors everywhere. Absolutely a woman's dream domain. Maybe she shouldn't have invited him inside. Had he never been inside a ladies' store before? Sweat dripped from his sandy hair, and he acted as if his shirt had suddenly grown too small.

She led him to a comfortable chair and edged him onto the white cushions. "Would you mind babysitting these shoes until I find the rest of the things I need?".

He nodded.

She loaded the two shoeboxes onto his lap.

A saleslady approached. "This way Miss, we have so many lovely wedding dresses. Do you prefer white, ivory, or a favorite color?

Charm turned her back and followed the saleslady. "I love traditional white. With a long, detachable train so I can dance at the reception."

A groan floated from the chair where Rick sat stiff and uncomfortable looking as if he were a pianist playing his first formal concert.

Was he sick? Maybe he really did like her. Maybe he didn't want her to find Harry and marry him. Her heart gave a little flutter, and she peeked over her shoulder at him. That kiss had exploded all her previous sessions with kissing any other men. Rick was dynamite. And he was so handsome. And so charmingly sweet sitting there looking uncomfortable. So like a boy being disappointed for wanting an air rifle when his mom gave him a yo-yo.

She glanced at the saleslady. "I'll look at your other clothes first. I lost my luggage and need to replenish for the remainder of my stay in Scotland."

The salesgirl nodded and headed her to a different part of the shop where she could no longer see Rick.

She lost track of time as she tried on dresses and jeans and sneakers. The shop carried a huge variety of smart outfits, so she chose four, plus jeans, a T-shirt, sneakers, panties, and bras, and another pair of yoga pants and T-shirt to sleep in.

As she tried each outfit, a picture of wearing the ensemble with a handsome man at her side invaded her thoughts. But the man wasn't Harry. The handsome, delightful, funny, and so helpful man was Rick. Thinking of him brought a smile to her lips and a bounce into her steps.

Charm strolled to the check-out counter and opened her purse. As she sorted through the clothes, the salesgirl tallied, wrapped, and stacked her purchases on the counter.

A clock chimed somewhere in the rear of the store. Five strokes. Closing time.

Charm sighed. The store had a beautiful selection of wedding dresses, but she'd run out of time. Maybe she didn't need a wedding dress. At least not here in Scotland. Maybe she'd find exactly what she wanted back in Tampa.

She smiled as she handed over her credit card. Leap Year was beginning to sound like a weird tradition. A woman shouldn't have to ask her man to marry her. He should be breaking the sound barrier to take her as her bride. Maybe she wouldn't search for Harry. Perhaps Rick was right. Harry wasn't that into her.

Charm gathered her purchases and moved to where she'd left Rick. "Here I am at last. Thank you for –"

A tall, stunning blonde with diamonds on her

wrists swept between where Charm stood to where Rick sat.

"Oh, darling! I knew you'd come as soon as you received my message. I've set our wedding day." She bent, cupped Rick's face, and gave him a long kiss.

CHAPTER 11

Charm stood frozen.

The woman prolonged the kiss and slid her sleek form down to perch on Rick's lap.

Like a lightning bolt Charm's feelings sent jagged shrapnel through her body. The woman was marrying Rick? Charm slammed her stunned mouth shut. And Rick had been coming on to her as if he planned to sweep her off her feet and carry her to his castle. As if she were the only woman in his life. Yet, he was going to marry this Miss Universe? Charm grabbed her packages in both arms. Just when was Rick planning to tell her? Pain ripped into her heart.

One box fell to the ground, then several others. Like pieces of her world were tumbling, they lay scattered at her feet. How could she have fallen so quickly for Rick? Why had he made her think he was available?

Charm bent, gathered her bundles, and tried to carry them all. She managed to juggle four boxes and two big bags, but several parcels still waited on the shining white counter.

She staggered to the door, but with her arms and hands full was unable to reach the doorknob.

Even if she fled outside, she couldn't get into that tiny car. Rick had locked the doors. There was no way to escape confronting him.

Her insides trembled. She'd fallen under Rick's spell. Even considered that marrying Harry might be a mistake. Realizing she really didn't want to marry a man she had to ask. Thinking she should return to Tampa and forget this silly dream of asking Harry.

Thinking she and Rick might have a future together. Falling in love.

She wedged a shoulder against the door as if she could bust her way outside. She'd go back to Tampa. Couldn't get there fast enough. Had to get away from Rick. But she was stranded here with him and that funny little car of his. She fought frustrated tears. Edinburgh had to be somewhere close. She'd catch the first flight back to Tampa. Maybe she'd find her sanity there.

How could that man treat her in the beautiful way he had when he was already up to his neck involved with a beautiful woman?

Tears pricked her eyelids. She blinked hard. She was stuck here with this double-dealing man. And her heart was breaking. She turned to glance at him, and her packages tumbled to the polished white tile in a new landslide.

Rick shoved and pushed to his feet.

The stunning blonde fell with a loud thump, hitting the floor with her pink-sheathed rump. "What …!" Her slender legs waved in the air. One designer shoe fell to either side. She grasped Rick's pant leg to keep from falling hard on her head.

Rick stumbled, lost his balance, and landed next to her on the polished tile floor. They lay twisted together like a pretzel.

Rick scrambled to release himself.

But the blonde entangled him with her arms and legs.

Despite herself, Charm laughed. Not funny the situation, but to watch those two scrambled on the floor of the posh shop with the three remaining customers gazing at them with open mouths ... just tickled her funny bone. Served him right, the gorgeous scamp. Nope, not a giggle coming from her mouth ... a sob.

Rick was the worst kind of two-timer. Stealing her heart from steady, reliable, yes, she'd admit the reality now, boring Harry. Then Rick shredding her feelings, her emotions, into confetti with another woman whom he'd no doubt charmed into his spider web of absolute attractive and perfect-seeming male.

She turned away from the two groveling on the floor and tried to retrieve her packages. Calm her pounding heart.

A man knelt beside her and gathered her parcels.

Where had he come from? She didn't care. "Thank you."

With his hands and arms full of her packages, he opened the door with a little finger on the knob and an elbow.

She rushed through into the fresh air and sunshine. Then glanced up and down the street. Now what? Brainiac was locked. She sure didn't want to get back into that little love-boat with Rick. She was done with Rick.

"How can I help you?" The soothing voice reminded her of the man standing at her side clutching her purchases.

"I don't suppose there is a taxi in this town?" Her voice quivered, but she didn't care.

"Actually, ma'am, I was waiting inside to take the lady … um the one writhing on the floor with the gentleman." He pointed to a black SUV with dark tinted windows. "My taxi is at your service."

Astounding. Really? "Can you drive me to Inverness?"

"Absolutely. No problem." He gave a sly smile. "I don't suppose you want to wait for the lady inside?"

"No. No. No. I don't. Or the gentleman either." She fumbled the back door open. "Just stuff my packages inside, and we can be on our way."

The tall, polite man bent and stowed all her packages in the back seat. Straightened and opened the front passenger door for her. "Inverness it is. Just a half hour away."

She glanced back at Kathleen's Bridal Shop. The door burst open, and Rick lunged halfway out with the blonde clinging to one arm and the back of his shirt like a barnacle on a ship under full sail.

Charm hopped into the passenger seat. "Hurry. Let's get out of here."

"Right." The driver was inside and stomping on the gas before she could take her eyes off Rick, still towing the blonde, struggling out the door toward her.

"Charm!"

His woeful voice followed them until engine noise obliterated his bellow.

CHAPTER 12

How glorious to be back home in Tampa. Charm kissed her fingertips to the baby blue sky. Her apartment welcomed her with open arms. She rushed into her own bedroom with its wide window overlooking the bay. How she needed to refresh herself with this aqua calmness of the waves brushing the shoreline.

But even more she needed to talk with Flurry. Find her way back to sanity. But Flurry wouldn't be home until tonight.

Charm tossed her overnight bag onto her fluffy white eiderdown quilt, unzipped the new suitcase, and started pulling out the trendy clothes she'd purchased at Kathleen's Bridal Shop. Tears started running down her cheeks. No. No. No. She wouldn't cry over a deceitful man. No more Rick in her life.

She rubbed a furious arm over her wet cheeks and hung her new clothes on hangers. Bright colors. Lovely textures. Styles just enough different from what she found in Tampa had seduced her into purchasing more than she'd needed. She'd expected to spend at least another week in Inverness. And she'd not looked at wedding dresses because she'd already decided not to propose to Harry. Realized that no, she actually didn't want to *ask* a man to marry her. But she'd hoped to spend some time with Harry. Remind him that she missed him. But definitely not use the Leap Year thing.

At least she had Rick to thank for opening her eyes. She liked to see the good in every situation, and Rick had exploded that leap year myth for her.

She deposited the lovely bridal shoes in the back of her closet on the highest shelf. Then stuck her feet into her soft pink slippers. Even after the two days her trip home had taken, her soles were still sore from hobbling on grass and tile until she stuck her feet into her new shoes at Kathleen's. Next time she traveled she'd wear comfortable shoes on the plane.

In her rush home, she hadn't had time to purchase new cosmetics, so she'd flown home with nothing but sunscreen on her face. She gazed out her apartment window. The flight arrived at Tampa International at 9:00 A.M., and she'd immediately retrieved her SUV and driven here in less than an hour. So, she had the whole day to fill. Maybe she would shop for cosmetics, get a mani and pedi, and call Flurry to meet for dinner tonight at *Our Place By The Sea.* Being home was great, but she needed to cheer herself up. She did not want to be alone.

She walked to the living room and switched on some music. Ice Cream. She needed ice cream. She strolled to the kitchen and opened her freezer door. Yep, there was Blue Bell. Her favorite Vanilla Bean. She scooped out four dips, added hot fudge and caramel topping, maraschino cherries, and chopped peanuts. Comfort food.

She opened the kitchen window, and the fresh bay breeze swept inside. August was a lovely month. A bit warm here, but so good to be back to weather she appreciated. No pouring rain. No mud. No beautiful man willing to carry her up a mountain. Ugh. That sad thought made her take a big bite of hot fudge smothered ice cream.

She spooned in another bite of topping-loaded ice cream. Mmmm. So Good. But she'd have to eat a lot more than this to fill the big, empty space in her heart.

Her cell rang.

"Hello."

Harry's voice. "Hi Sweetheart."

"Harry? Where are you?"

"Home."

Her heart bucked. "How long have you been here?"

"One day, and I've got to see you."

Charm put her palm over the speaker. Really? Okay, she didn't want to be alone, but did she want to see Harry? Was she really ready to face him? How could he be back in Tampa?

"I have a surprise for you."

Surprise? His being here almost knocked her off her feet. "I thought you planned to be in Scotland at least two more months." Ironic, she'd just spent a fruitless week tramping that country trying to find him.

"I have the weekend off, and I want to see you."

"Well, yes, of course."

"Tonight at 8:00. We'll meet at your favorite spot. *Our Place By The Sea.*"

"That would be lovely."

"You don't sound excited."

"You surprised me, that's all." She hesitated, then swallowed. "Tonight at 8:00 then."

~

Charm strolled into the elegant dining room just off the more casual patio restaurant at *Our Place By The Sea.* She glanced around. Most of the white-clothed tables were already filled with well-dressed couples. The men wore what in Tampa was considered formal, a collared-sport shirt and a sports coat. The women wore off-the-shoulder dresses, and jewelry sparkled at tanned necks and wrists. Upswept hair styles displayed diamond earrings.

She wore one of the dresses she'd purchased at Kathleen's Bridal Shop, an off one-shoulder strapless. Her white dress had a full skirt swinging above those adorable pink heels also bought at Kathleen's. Certainly, she and Kathleen had similar tastes in clothes ... and men. Charm shook her head, ejecting that thought from her mind.

"May I seat you, Miss Clearbell?"

"Oh, hello Larry. Aren't you usually in the casual dining area?"

"Yes. But we had a full house here in the Crystal Room at the last-minute tonight, so I volunteered to help out."

"That was sweet of you, Larry. I'm glad you're here. I may need a friendly face. This could turn out to be a rather awful evening."

"Sorry to hear that. You've been away for a few days I understand."

"Yes, almost a week. Scotland. Lovely land. Lovely people … for the most part. But the weather can turn bad without notice … and … seems life can change on an ill wind as well." Charm swallowed a sob.

Larry bowed. "I hope your evening tonight turns out much better than you expect. Mr. Bear has reserved the special table at the window in the center of the room. The one covered with roses."

Charm followed the waiter to the table set on a dais above the room. As Larry pulled out her chair, the sweet scent of roses met her.

"Thank you, Larry." She sank into the chair, suddenly tired from her hurried trip home.

Larry filled her glass with ice water, then silently disappeared.

Charm smiled. Some lady must be a happy wife married to that man. She gazed around the candle-lit room. Really crowded for a weeknight. Was her imagination playing tricks or were some of the ladies at the other tables peeking over menus to gaze at her? She glanced out the window at the sloop riding a gentle wave far below, its white sides glistening in the moonlight. Moonbeam sparkles danced across the gentle waves. Stars twinkled in the sky. Such a perfect night.

She tapped her fingers on the white cloth. Harry was late. Again. The man always had to make an entrance. What could his surprise be? Hopefully, no more diamond earrings. Perhaps he wanted to tell her that the fifty-four-foot sloop docked outside was his. And he wanted to pressure her into spending her weekend with him.

Well, tonight would be the end. Either he proposed ... or she broke up with the man. She had given him a year of her life. Either –

"Hello, darling. You look absolutely lovely."

Charm started.

Harry bent and kissed her cheek, rounded the table, and plunged into his seat. "I hope you love the flowers and the table." He nodded to Larry. "Bring the champagne please."

Charm smiled. "Well I—"

"Darling, I had a most profitable time in Scotland. Great land that. But you would not believe how much I missed you." He leaned across the table and clasped both her hands. "The women there are not so eager to have facial work done. They prefer the 'natural attributes God gave them.' Even the students I'm teaching are more interested in surgery to correct malformities than plastic surgery to display hidden beauty. All that is rather boring, but I shall return and complete my two months teaching responsibilities. However, ..."

Harry sprang from his chair and gazed around the room. "I've invited a number of my friends and patients tonight to share this momentous occasion." He nodded to the people seated at the other tables.

Heads nodded back. Smiles appeared. A gentle applause rippled around the dining room.

Harry waved to them.

"These are your friends?" Charm lifted her napkin. If only she could hide behind the small cloth.

"Yes, darling." Harry gazed around the room, his handsome head nodding to this guest and that as if he were in his home welcoming his friends to a formal dinner.

Then he came to stand beside her.

She gazed wide-eyed as he lowered himself to his knees at her side.

An orchestra started playing.

He reached for her hand.

A spotlight flashed on, and numerous cell phones clicked pictures. Somewhere near the rear of the restaurant, a flash revealed a large professional camera.

Harry reached inside his tux jacket and removed a tiny box. He opened the box and held the contents under her gaze.

A huge emerald-cut diamond ring.

Charm's hand flew to her mouth.

CHAPTER 13

Rick stalked over to the tall, white-haired waiter. "Do you know a Miss Charm Clearbell?"

"Yes, sir. She's a regular here."

"I'm way out of my comfort zone here, but I've travelled four thousand one hundred seventy-nine miles with two plane changes from Scotland to find the lady. I don't have her address or phone number, but I do know she frequents this restaurant. I'll be sitting here at a table day and night until she comes. I wanted to alert you so you wouldn't think I was checking the place for a robbery or trying to pick up ladies. I have only one special lady I really, really need to see.

"I'm Larry. I can contact her to let her know you're wanting to see her."

Rick frowned. "No. Please don't. I'm not sure Charm ever wants to see me again." He backed up to one of the tall tables that looked over the water. "I'm Rick McDougal. I'll just park here until she comes. Just bring me a coffee will you please?"

"I'll bring your coffee. I trust you don't have any intention of hurting the lady. Correct?"

Rick glanced down at his worn jeans and rumpled long-sleeved shirt. He rubbed his hand over the two-days growth on his face. "Maybe I should have gone home and cleaned up first. But no, the lady means the world to me, and I would never hurt her."

Larry rubbed his chin. Then the back of his neck. Then he ran his hand through his hair. Then he straightened his shoulders as if he'd just made a decision. "You believe in God, McDougal?"

"Absolutely. I believe God sent His Son as my Savior."

"Do you believe God has a plan for our lives?"

Rick smiled and relaxed in his chair. Just like God to send a friend when he most needed one. "Yes, as long as we ask for His will and try to obey Him, I believe He has a plan for my life."

"Then get ready for a shock, McDougal. Miss Charm Clearbell is seated in the next room. If you walk in, I'm sure you'll locate her."

Rick sprang up from the chair and grabbed Larry's arm. "Thanks man." He tucked in his shirt. Probably should have zipped home and cleaned up, but he hadn't taken the time, He'd tailed her taxi until he lost the cab at the airport. Found the driver again as the taxi was exiting and pounded the guy with questions until the driver confessed that he'd driven Charm directly to the American departure gate. Rick heaved a sigh. Then he hopped on the first flight to the US.

If he'd waited to shower, he might have missed her tonight.

He put his hand on the interior door. *Oh Father God, please don't let me blow this. I'm sure this is the woman I've been looking for my whole life. So,*

I'm trusting this meeting tonight is Your will. You know she's a feisty, independent lady, and she thinks she's in love with another man, so I really need You on my side here. In Jesus' powerful name, Amen.

He opened the door.

Charm!

And all but fell through. His hand on the knob held him upright.

A table stood on the dais of the large, candlelit room. A light spotlighted the table. A man on his knees held what could only be, judging by the sparkles shooting from the object, an enormous diamond ring. The suave man wore a full tux and appeared tall and well-built. His face was turned halfway toward the woman and the other half toward the diners oohing and aahing from various tables.

The woman seated and gazing down was –

Yes, it was her. Rick's knees turned to water. He slid down to crouch on his haunches. He hadn't been mistaken. "Charm."

His whispered word didn't carry over the crowd's murmurs.

~

The diamond sparkled and glittered. Charm swallowed. So beautiful. She gazed down into Harry's wide-eyed gaze and grasped her hands tightly in her lap. Two weeks ago, she had desired this ring with all her heart. She'd been devastated when Harry had given her the diamond earrings instead. For almost a year, she'd been dreaming that she would one day become Mrs. Harry Bear. Wife to a highly respected surgeon. She'd even followed him to Scotland with the insane thought of offering Harry a Leap Year proposal.

She had thought that she loved him. Did she?

Harry's blue gaze morphed from highly confident to a slight question. He nudged the ring box closer.

Then she met Rick. The man was so obnoxious.

Until she got to know him a little.

Then he gave up his bed for her. And turned out to be funny. And helpful. And thoughtful. And caring. And spontaneous. And oh, so sexy. And that one kiss!

"Charm?" Harry's eyes held big questions and red tinged his cheeks.

Harry was predictable. And safe. Yet none of Harry's kisses, roses, and gifts compared to that single kiss in the Scottish wilderness.

Harry was loaded with money. Which *was* nice.

If she judged Rick by his clothes and car, he probably didn't have a cent to his name. Although Care Pilots probably made a livable income.

Harry's irritated voice broke into her thoughts. "Charm. My knees are giving out. Come on, quit the theatrics. Take the ring. Say yes."

She closed her eyes. But Rick belonged to someone else.

And Harry wanted her. She opened her eyes, leaned down and cupped Harry's smooth cheeks in both her hands. "Dear Harry, I'm so very fond of you. I even thought I loved you."

Harry stumbled to his feet. "Then take the ring." He thrust the beauty toward her.

"I'm so sorry. I can't marry you."

"What?" The words exploded from Harry's lips. "But Mother insists ... "

The newsman's flash exploded. Murmurs from the tables grew to rumbles.

Harry motioned to someone, and the spotlight clicked off.

He grabbed her shoulder, squeezed, and stuck his face close to hers. "Don't ever embarrass me like this again. Of course, you'll marry me. I'll give you more time. I sprang this on you, and you're surprised that's all." He stood over her, breathing in her face, his eyes blazing.

Charm tried to push his hand away. "You're hurting me. Please let go."

"You heard the lady. Take your hands off her."

Charm stiffened. That voice. Impossible. It couldn't be. "Rick?"

Harry dropped his hands.

Rick here? Fabulous man. But had he spent the last two days living in a trash bin? His shirt was as rumpled as a hobo's, and a heavy shadow darkened his cheeks. He looked much as he had the first time she'd seen him at the Fraserburg Diner. Especially the scowl on his face.

But her heart fluttered, warmed, and thrilled.

Until the image of the blonde at the bridal shop flashed in her mind. This long day had ended even worse than she'd expected. She rose. "If you two men will excuse me, I've had a long and difficult day."

"You stay put. I'll be back!" Harry looked down his nose at her, targeted a I'm richer-smarter-and-better-looking-than-you stare at Rick, spun on his highly polished dress shoes, then walked with a swift, marching pace toward the men's room.

Charm pulled in a deep breath. Watching his tall figure swagger across the room, a load slid from her shoulders. How had she not noticed what an arrogant man Harry was?

She rushed to the exit door as fast as her pretty high heels would take her.

CHAPTER 14

Charm hurried down the dock toward her SUV. How could Rick possibly be here? He was in Scotland making plans to marry that blonde.

She'd almost reached her SUV when his voice called, echoing over the soft sound of the waves on the pier and the rumble of distant traffic.

"Charm, wait. Please. I don't know where you live."

She shook her head. The man was crazy. He'd flown thousands of miles to see her, and he didn't even know where she lived! She hesitated in front of her car, her palm on the handle. *Father, God, how did he find me?*

And why would he follow her? He was supposed to marry that other woman. She found herself really disliking the sensational blonde.

Okay, Rick was here. In Tampa. She owed him enough to listen to his explanation. She moved from her car to the end of the pier where an iron bench stood looking out toward the bay. She settled on the iron seat and watched him running to her.

"Thank God I found you." He stood next to her, hands on his knees, taking in big breaths.

The sound of his voice sent warmth to her

heart. She didn't invite him to sit. Didn't trust him so close. The mere sight of him had her entire body tingling.

"That was Harry Bear?" The gold flecks in Rick's brown eyes shown in the soft moonlight.

"Yes."

"You refused his ring? His proposal?"

"Yes."

Rick stood straighter, arching his back, breathing long breaths. "I couldn't hear from where I stood. No more Leap Year proposal?"

"No."

"May I sit?"

She patted the iron seat. "Do."

He dropped a long leg over the bench and sat sideways, facing her, one leg on either side. "I'd like to explain about the woman."

"I'd love for you to."

"Her name is Kathleen. The bridal shop is hers. She's usually not there on Wednesdays. I don't know why she was there that day."

"I'm glad she was." Charm turned from him to gaze out over the restless water sloshing the shoreline. "I discovered you already had a woman in your life. Do you have many more?"

"I know what that scene looked like, but it wasn't anywhere near that."

"You set a wedding date?"

"No. Absolutely not." He leaned toward her and touched her hand. "I had one single date with Kathleen. Believe me. One date."

"It appeared as if she knew you quite well."

"No. We went to a movie. I drove her home."

Rick took her hand. "Nothing more."

She left her hand between his warm ones. Hot actually, from the night air and his run. But she didn't care. Rumpled, hot, and sweaty, her heart soared. Rick was here. Sitting beside her. What more could she ask for? "But she thinks you're going to marry her?"

"She's kooky. I had already decided not to date her again. That night after the movie, she invited me to her home. She wanted to talk. I'm a gentleman so I agreed."

Rick scooted closer, held her hands more firmly as if he thought she might spring up and run again. "Okay, I know this is going to sound strange, but hear me out."

Charm nodded. Oh, this man was the most intense man she'd ever met. And she dearly loved intensity.

"To start with, my four friends that you met at the diner set me up on the date with her. They figured Kathleen was attractive enough to keep me in Scotland so the diner would stay open."

"Makes sense. She is quite lovely."

"We sat on her couch. Unfortunately, she perched directly beneath a reading light which she'd left on when we went on our date. The light cast a full spotlight on her face. I noticed she appeared to be older than I'd thought. A good bit older. Her hands gave her away. I'd guess she'd had plastic surgery to keep her looks."

"Oh?"

"Of course, my friends wouldn't have known about her age. Or her obsession."

"She wanted a husband?"

"No. She didn't want a husband. She'd had one of those and evidently, he was abusive, so she discarded him."

"What *did* she want?"

"My genes. She liked my looks, so she wanted me to father a baby with her."

"Wow!"

"Yeah. I didn't wait to hear any more, I tore out of there like a hare from a hound."

"But—"

"She badgered me. Sent emails, letters, visited me at the diner, sent thugs to threaten me." Rick squeezed her hands. "And tackled me at the bridal shop."

Charm's heart beat furiously. "Now what?"

"I'm here and she's in Scotland." His hand closed on hers and gave a tug. "Let's go back inside and have dinner. I haven't eaten since I left Scotland. I'm so hungry my stomach's pushing my backbone, and I doubt you've eaten."

Charm jumped up. peeked at him. "Starved."

He held her hand as they walked the pier back to *Our Place By The Sea.* "Casual or Crystal Room?"

"Either."

Larry approached, a wide grin on his face. "Sorry, the patio is full. I have one table available in the Crystal Room. Follow me."

"Not the one on the dais."

"Oops sorry. But Mr. Bear booked that one for the evening. He left. It's the only table available."

"We'll take it." Rick guided her to the seat she

had occupied earlier across from Harry.

She hesitated a second then slid into the chair. The roses still scented the air. The candlelight around them cast a soft glow. "You're probably the only man who has ever eaten in this room dressed like he just hopped off a hobo train."

Rick laughed. "Let's celebrate. Larry, we'll have champaign and lobsters. That is if the lady likes lobsters."

"Love them. But there're pretty expensive here. I can pay my share."

"I'm buying. We won't quibble about the bill."

Larry left to get their order.

Without warning Rick rose, moved to her side, and slid to his knees.

"What?" Charm giggled. Rick looked so sweet. On his knees, hair tousled, clothes rumpled, sleeves folded to the elbow, so unlike any of the other patrons.

"Charm." He took her hand, his face serious. "I'm so in love with you, I can't breathe without you, let alone live without you. Would you do me the honor of becoming my best friend, the love of my life, and my wife?" He reached into his pocket and pulled out a tiny box. He opened the box to display a diamond.

Charm giggled. Rick was asking her … her giggles stopped. He was serious. She glanced at the ring. Then gazed into his shining brown eyes. Her mouth answered before she knew what she said. "Oh, yes." But her heart knew.

"You made me a different man. Better. You made me see the world through a new lens. I'm like a kid again. You made me laugh until my stomach hurt. I marveled that I'd stopped seeing beauty around me. Felt like I'd been walking through my life in a fog … until you blew the vapor away. With every hour we spent together, I became more sure I wanted to enjoy the rest of my life with you."

He slipped the ring on her finger.

The diners at the surrounding tables clapped!

Maybe they weren't as good friends of his as Harry thought.

She stood then, and for several seconds, neither of them moved. And then they both did, both at once, and she was in his arms, and he was kissing her.

He was sweetness and fire, kissing so fiercely, that her heart nearly exploded in her chest.

When he finally pulled away, breathless and dizzy, she was laughing and maybe crying a little. "I've never done anything even remotely like this. I just … I don't do this."

He stopped her with another kiss.

The world paused. This was why God made man and woman. This joy of being together. This sharing. This looking forward to a lifetime of knowing and loving one another.

And he did have superb genes.

The kiss ended too soon when Larry popped the cork on the bubbly. "Imagine two proposals in one night. Miss Clearbell, you've won the lottery."

"Yes, I have, Larry. I have."

They sat, staring into one another's eyes as Larry poured the champagne.

Larry cleared his throat. "Have you heard the

tale of *Our Place By The Sea*? When you meet a man for the first time here, you will fall in love, get married, and live happily ever after. I'd say that applies to the two of you."

Charm giggled. "Oh yes, it does."

Rick winked. "Why do you think I waited *here* to find Charm?" He handed her a glass to celebrate with.

She didn't need any champagne. She was tipsy in love with Rick.

I hope you enjoyed TIPSY FOR LOVE as much as I had fun writing this latest book. Here is the first chapter of my book,

A SMALL VOICE.
CHAPTER 1

Piper McCormack blinked. "What? What did you just say? I can't date him."

"I worked a long time to set up this date." Jessica curled her model-thin legs beneath her on the couch, and her pretty face lit with her you're-my-best-friend smile. "So, spill-it. Why can't you date the dreamy doctor I set you up with?"

"I didn't know my blind date was an OBGYN."

"I told you he was a doctor." Jessica's eyes widened. "You're not pregnant, are you?"

Piper shook her head. "You've got an active imagination. Who would be the father? I haven't dated in …" She tilted her head. "I've been too busy during the last four months. Not since Jason, and we never had much going. No, I'm not expecting a baby." She patted her flat stomach.

"Okay, why are you so upset to discover your date's an OBGYN?"

Piper dropped her head and sighed, then she smiled. "I don't usually share my story. Are you sure you want to know?"

"Oh yeah, you've got me hooked. What secret are you hiding?"

"If you hadn't set me up with this blind date, I'd never share. I don't want to scare you away because of my peculiar view on life."

"Are you a witch? A vampire? A werewolf?"

"You've watched too many horror movies." Piper settled on her cushy, white armchair, picked up her hot chocolate, and sipped. The artificial flames in her marble fireplace crackled.

"Oh, this has to be good! Come on, tell me what makes you so different from all the rest of us. Not that I've noticed any big diversity between you and my other friends, except you're such a put-together, self-assured, Miss Have-Your-Life-Planned-To-One-Hundred lady."

Piper laughed. She jumped from her chair, circled the coffee table, leaned down, and hugged Jessica. "You are so wrong. On every point." She hugged Jessica again. "You're so upbeat. Maybe that's one reason I think you're incredible."

"Not me. I'm your every-day average big-city Texas girl, though I don't have big hair or wear cowboy boots. You couldn't pick me out of dozens walking the streets of Dallas."

Piper giggled. "No one downtown has big hair or wears cowboy boots."

"No, but I've been told they used to." Jessica tossed her long curly hair over her shoulder, revealing the tiny rose tattooed on the side of her neck.

Piper stepped back to her seat, shuffling her bare feet deep into her white carpet, which usually made her feel like she could tackle anything that came her way. Not tonight. She only shared her story when pressed. Telling left her in such an emotionally vulnerable place.

She'd made a new start in Dallas. Moved here because of her high-powered job and had discovered Texans really were big-hearted, accepting people. She'd remain nestled in their friendliness the rest of her life. So far, she'd not lost any friends when pressed to tell her story, and she didn't want to alienate Jessica.

They shared the same glass-walled office on Ross Avenue and would one day be competitors for the boss's job. She admired Jessica, who had been a straight-shooter in office politics and more fun away from work during girls' night out than any other person Piper had met. So, telling Jessica was hard.

Piper settled on the couch, tugged a throw pillow over her chest, and pulled in a deep breath. "Okay. I doubt you've ever met anyone like me. There are so few of us. But here's the thing – I'm an abortion survivor."

Jessica's big brown eyes stared, then blinked. "What?"

"Forty-seven years ago, the Supreme Court handed down the decision meant to be my death sentence." Piper let that sink in for a full thirty seconds.

"You … you survived. How?"

"I don't blame my birth mother for having an abortion. She was thirteen-years-old and had been raped."

"Oh, no!" Jessica jammed her hand over her heart. "My adoptive parents told me my birth mother's mother bundled her off to an abortion clinic where my biological mother underwent a saline abortion. For five days, I soaked in a toxic salt solution being poisoned and scalded. But the abortion was unsuccessful."

"How could you have survived?"

"I had a twin. She didn't survive. After she was born, the doctor thought he'd completed the abortion. A month after, my birth mother continued to have pregnancy signs, but the doctor believed the morning sickness was psychological. Three more months passed, and the signs became obvious my birth mother was still pregnant, but she refused another abortion, and chose to put me up for adoption."

"Wow! That took courage. I'm sorry to be so dumb, but I know almost nothing about abortions. What is a saline abortion?"

"A saline abortion is different from most abortions because the procedure takes longer." Piper squeezed her eyes shut and tried to block out graphic pictures that formed in her mind whenever she told her story. "The doctor injects the solution into the baby's amniotic fluid and the solution surrounds the baby and is supposed to burn her to death. The murder can take hours and hours to work. If the abortion happens late enough in the pregnancy, a few babies accidentally survive, and are born alive."

"What happens to them?"

"The doctor or nurse throws the baby into the

garbage can and lets the child die."

Jessica raced for the bathroom. When she returned several minutes later, her complexion had paled. She slid down on the plush sofa and drew herself into a huddle.

Piper noticed her hand shook when she lifted her hot chocolate. "I'm sorry to burden you with my story. I just need you to understand why I can't possibly date the OB you set me up with." She took a sip. Already cold. Like her heart was to the idea of dating a possible abortionist. Here she was overreacting again, but she tended to go hyper more often than she liked. Probably another scar from the attempted abortion.

Jessica's chilled hand squeezed hers. "I think you and I are best friends now." Her pretty forehead furrowed into a frown. "But I can't call off the date. Dr. Connors is coming straight from the airport to your apartment, and he's turned off his mobile as he does when he's not on call. I can't reach him. He'll be here in..." she glanced at her cell "... three hours."

Piper's shoulders slumped. Destiny. Her small voice had warned, she would meet this doctor. For what reason, she did not know. "Excuse me, Jessica. I'll be right back."

Piper dragged her bare feet through the luxurious carpet, but the warmth didn't reach her heart. Didn't give her courage. She entered her bedroom and dropped to sit on the edge of her bed.

"What will happen when the doc and I meet, my dear twin. I know you only glimpse the future, but I so wish you'd tell me," she whispered into the darkness.

No tiny voice answered.

ANNE GREENE BIO

My home is in the quaint antiquing town of McKinney, Texas, just a few miles north of Dallas. My dear husband is a retired Colonel, Army Special Forces. My little blonde and white Shih Tzu, Lily Valentine, shares my writing space, curled at my feet. I have four beautiful, talented children, and eight grandchildren who keep me on my toes.

I've lived in or traveled to every location of each book I've written, and each book is a book of my heart. Besides my first love, writing, I enjoy travel, art, reading, movies, and way too many other things to mention. Life is good. Jesus said, "I am come that you might have life and that you might have it more abundantly." Whether writing contemporary or historical, my books celebrate the abundant life Jesus gives.

If you're an electronic reader, CLICK ON THE FOLLOWING LINKS to learn about my other books. If you are a print book reader, you will find all my books listed on my website, http://www.AnneGreeneAuthor.com or on Amazon.com.

Trail of Tears: The Story of John Ross
Shadow of the Dagger
Angel with Steel Wings
Red is for Rookie

Masquerade Marriage
Marriage By Arrangement
A Texas Christmas Mystery
A Christmas Belle (Christmas Mail Order Angels)
The California Gold Rush Romance Collection: 9 Stories of Finding Treasures Worth More than Gold
Keara's Escape (A Spinster Orphan Train novella)
Daredevils
Spur of the Moment Bride
An Undaunted Matchmaker
Hatteras Island Mystery
Recipe for a Husband
One Groom is Not Enough
A Groom for Christmas
Avoiding the Mistletoe
A Rebel Spy
The Choice
Lord Bentley Needs A Bride
Mystery at Dead Broke Ranch
Her Reluctant Hero
Dollar Brides
A Crazy Optimist
Texas Law
Lacy and the Law
Brides of the Wild West
Love at Christmas
A Small Voice
A Williamsburg Christmas
Mistletoe, Jingle Bells, and Second Chances (4 book series)
Days Gone By: Christian Historical Romance Collection
Brides Go West: Two historical novellas
Anne Greene Author Home Page
Anne Greene's Books on Amazon

Made in the USA
Monee, IL
14 September 2023